down with the SICKNESS
and Other Chilling Tales

Gabriella Balcom

www.darkmythpublications.com/

Dark Myth Publications, a division of
The JayZoMon/Dark Myth Company, LLC.
21050 Little Beaver Rd, Apple Valley, CA 92308

ISBN: 979-8-9863807-2-8

First Printing November 2022

Dark Myth Publications is a registered trademark of The JayZoMon Dark Myth Company, LLC.

10 9 8 7 6 5 4 3 2 1

Table of Contents

*I dedicate this book
to my precious children.
You are my heroes
—always have been—
and I love you very much.
Don't ever give up.
Keep trying, no matter what,
and remember you're not alone.*

Introduction

I never dreamed I'd write horror, but I do, and I love it. Let me start at the beginning, though.

Where the Wild Things Are took me by surprise when I first tried to read it. It terrified me. I was three years old then and growing up in a bad situation. My father was abusive; my mother was passive and didn't take any action to protect me. I felt genuine fear many times, never knew what would happen next, and I guess I just couldn't handle anything that generated similar feelings.

Even though I shied away from stories that seemed scary, my parents took me to see scary movies now and then. *Jaws* horrified me so much that my memories remain fresh, as if they're from yesterday. For weeks, I *knew* something was under my bed. I avoided darkness and shadows, kept several feet away from my bed, and my heart raced when I looked at it. At bedtime, I'd jump onto it from a distance, and the following morning, I'd leap from it and run off as fast as I could.

My terror eventually waned, and I found other spooky things intriguing. I came to adore Poe, along with authors like Wells, Bradbury, Shelley, Doyle, Stevenson, Herbert, Rice, Saul, Morrell, Koontz, Stine, and King. However, it never occurred to me to try my own hand at anything dark.

I did my first "writing," per se, when I was two — lists of animals, plants, and trees beginning with the letters of the alphabet. Soon after, I began creating short stories, followed by journaling a few years later, then composing poetry.

But I stopped writing altogether after I went to college. Work, school, and life kept me busy, along with marriage and children. Divorcing my husband and becoming a single parent had me even busier. I wrote the occasional work-related article, but nothing else. However, ideas had always popped into my head, and never stopped. I finally reached a point in 2012 where I couldn't keep the floodgates shut any longer. Words poured out of me. Initially, my writing was cathartic, but it turned creative. I wrote fantasy, sci-fi, romance, literary fiction, children's stories, and more. To my surprise, horror also flowed from me. My characters were as real to me as you and I are, and their stories made me shiver. They still do.

Horror means a great deal to me, and to hundreds of thousands across the world. It allows me to release strong emotions like pain, think clearly, and quite literally fills me with hope. It shakes me and makes my breath catch in my throat. It opens the door to any number of fantastical possibilities, hurtling me straight toward them. Our day-to-day reality isn't all that exists. Karma is real. Evil is, too, but it can be defeated. The inexplicable occurs every day, and unknown things are really out there, both the good and the bad. Don't you feel them? I do.

I wish you a world of wonder, both terrifying and utterly amazing. Also, I very much hope you enjoy my collection of stories.

Gabriella Balcom
October, 2022

down with the SICKNESS
and Other Chilling Tales

—

 **Down with the Sickness**

BREATHING FASTER, CRYSTAL stared at the TV screen. She was mesmerized, unable to tear her eyes away.

John Mayer, whom she idolized, was performing in a benefit concert. Grabbing her guitar, she accompanied him. He, Justin Bieber, and her other rock idols were the very reason she'd begun playing and singing in the first place, and she knew their songs by heart.

Cheering with the audience later, she imagined them yelling for her.

The next day

Crystal plucked the strings on her guitar and strummed, stopping briefly to jot down notes. Words popped into her head, and her breath sped up as she wrote, because they were dynamite lyrics. The melody was pretty nice, too.

Half an hour later, though, she grimaced. Despite feeling inspired previously, she hadn't come up with anything else since then—at least, nothing worthwhile. Something tantalizing floated around the edges of her mind, teasing her, but it eluded her when she tried to pin it down. She tried again and again but was unsuccessful every time. Frustration and anger welled up inside her and she glared at her guitar, throwing it. She flinched when it landed on the floor with a loud *thunk*. It dawned on her the guitar could've cracked or been damaged in another way, but she just shrugged and glanced around her room.

Her video games caught her eye. Turning her attention to her favorite, Need for Speed, she lost herself in it within moments. Racing here, there, and everywhere, all the while dodging obstacles, she finished fifth in one race, second in the next. In the third, though, she crashed before reaching the finish line, and several cars passed her. She lost the next game soundly and cursed under her breath.

A riff suddenly ran through her mind, one she thought good enough to bring people out of their seats screaming, and giddy laughter bubbled inside her. She snatched up her guitar and began playing but scowled when she fumbled on the notes. Staring at her hands, she wished they were bigger, more agile, more flexible, something. Her reach was a problem—always had been—and sometimes she rushed, making mistakes on easy stuff.

Recalling instances, she'd visited with her friends or done other things instead of practicing, she felt twinges of guilt, but ignored them. Surely she'd more than made up for slacking by working longer and harder other times.

Crystal's phone chimed and she leaned her guitar against a wall. Her best friend, Roxie, had sent her a link and she gasped after clicking it.

She sprinted from her room, taking the stairs down to the first floor two at a time, and looked for her parents. Mom wasn't anywhere to be found, but Dad was paring potatoes in the kitchen.

"This is what I want for my birthday," she blurted out, voice quivering with excitement. Barely able to contain herself, she held up her cell phone for him to see. Excitement and anticipation hummed through her veins.

Her father studied the pictured Les Paul guitar and raised his eyebrows. He looked at her a few seconds before responding. "You told us what you wanted months ago, and your Mom and I put it on layaway."

Crystal shrugged. "I don't want that stuff anymore."

All she could think of was the Les Paul. It was the fanciest one she'd ever seen, sparkly with varying shades of purple, and she knew she'd be a success if she had it. She'd play better than ever before. Everyone would be envious, and no one would be able to take their eyes off her.

"You don't *want* the layaway?" Dad stared at her as if she'd grown an extra head. "Those things cost over $600, and we've been making payments on them all this time."

"But I don't..."

He put his hands on his hips, frowning. "Money doesn't grow on trees, young lady. Your mother and I aren't rich, and we work hard for our wages. That is nothing but a guitar. It's not clothing you can wear all year. Not the contacts you've been asking for. Not the dental checkup and cleaning you've needed for months now, not to mention your cavity needs to be addressed. And that

3

guitar's not the computer you've hounded us to buy for months. Remember telling us how much you needed it for research and typing up assignments?"

"A Les Paul isn't *just* a guitar, Dad. Justin Bieber has one. John Mayer has *several*. William Duvall and Jerry Cantrell do, too. Lots of famous people have them, and I need..."

"Stop right there. I'm tired of hearing about rock stars and guitar players, and all the things they have that you want. They aren't gods or God's gift to the world either. They're humans like you and me, and you don't need to own what they do. You'll be eighteen next month and you're about to start your last year of high school. You need to get your head out of the clouds and focus on what matters—finishing the twelfth grade, going on to college, and working toward a real career."

"Music *is* a real career."

"Maybe for some people, but not you." Dad's voice was flat.

Tears sprang to Crystal's eyes. "Why can't you believe in me? Mom does. She's always supportive."

He sighed, taking her by the shoulders. "I do believe in you, Honey, but people who are determined to achieve their dreams bust their butts to reach them. I'm sure someday you'll find something you want badly enough to work for it."

"Singing and playing the guitar *are* what I want," she argued. "And I practice them."

"I'm not trying to be negative but doing things only a little before stopping isn't my idea of hard work. You spend time with your guitar, but never long, and sometimes not

4

for days. You're always texting friends, going to movies or eating out with them, watching TV, or playing games instead of spending time with your guitar. Or you look for easier ways to master stuff instead of doing it the old-fashioned way that requires time, repetition, and hard work."

"I do work hard," she insisted, but she looked away from his steady gaze.

"Crystal, I love you very much, and I think you can do anything you put your mind to. But you have to be determined and committed to doing what it takes to succeed. Dreams and wishes don't fall into our laps. We have to do our share."

"I really want the guitar," she stressed, changing the subject. "*Please* get it for me, Dad."

"We don't have several thousand dollars for a guitar. That's more than what we need to redo the kitchen floor." Part of theirs had begun dry rotting because of leaky pipes, and they'd been told the damaged flooring would have to be replaced, along with underlying beams. Since they didn't have the money, the family had temporarily stacked cinder blocks underneath the problem areas instead. "And my truck's got an oil leak we have to deal with soon. That could turn out to be a blown head gasket, or something worse."

"But I *need* it."

"No, you don't. You don't need a specific instrument to do well. If being a musician means that much to you, practice on the guitar you have."

"It's no good, not like the..."

"*What?*" he snapped. "Don't let me hear you say that

5

again. Your guitar cost us several hundred dollars, money we could've put to good use on other things, and here you are calling it trash. If I'd known you'd have this attitude, I wouldn't have agreed to get it for you. And I know your mother would agree."

Crystal remembered how her parents had made payments on that, too, and regretted her rash words. "I'm sorry, Dad." But she imagined herself holding the Les Paul —playing it and people cheering—and wanted it more than anything. "I could do so much with the guitar I showed you, and I'll put money toward it."

"You don't have any money. You quit your job, remember?"

"I'll get another. You and Mom can buy the guitar and I'll make payments to you until I've paid you off."

"If you want it, get a job and save up for it."

"That'll take forever," Crystal argued. "I want it now."

"You'll do fine without that expensive thing." Dad squeezed her shoulder. "And, if you really want it, get another job like I said, and start saving."

That night, she sulked after talking with Mom. Her mother had encouraged her to pursue her goals and dreams, but she'd agreed with Crystal's father that they wouldn't buy the guitar.

One month later

"Look," Roxie said, pointing. "I want a voodoo doll."

Crystal grimaced, looking at Voodoo Land, the shop across the street from them. She wished she had more money, because a voodoo doll would be a great souvenir to take home, and she'd been longing to have one. But ever since she'd talked about not wanting her birthday items which were on layaway, her parents had been acting differently. They'd insisted on her doing chores around the house without fail, rather than letting her slide on them now and then as they'd done before. And they'd been very stingy with money. They'd stopped slipping her the occasional five-dollar bill like they used to, and Mom had been uncharacteristically stern, telling Crystal a few times that she should appreciate what she had, rather than focusing on things she didn't have and didn't need. They'd even stopped her allowance, saying it wouldn't resume until she showed some responsibility and got a job.

She'd found one pretty fast and saved up $135 for her band trip to New Orleans—where she and Roxie were now —but wasn't happy about it. Listening to the other girl chattering about all the amazing things she planned to buy, Crystal couldn't help but wish she had her friend's parents. They hadn't given their daughter a hard time about money or nagged her to get a job; instead, they'd just handed over $400 as "spending money," telling her to have fun.

While Roxie eagerly examined the dozens of dolls, spells, hexes, and charms, Crystal wandered around the shop. She was browsing through a rack of t-shirts when she noticed a small sign on the wall reading *"Make your dreams come true."*

"I was homeless once," a man with a deep voice said quietly. "It was long ago."

Crystal flinched, eyes widening because she hadn't seen him there. A few feet away, he stood underneath a bright light, which shone into her eyes, blinding her. She blinked a couple times, trying to make out his features, but couldn't.

"My father kicked me out of our home," he continued. "Most of my family rejected me, and I had nothing. No car. No home. No money. But now I have all that, and much, much more."

She listened, intrigued, and watched him approach. Finally able to see him, she studied his handsome, striking features, cobalt-blue eyes, and impeccably styled hair. His elegant, dark blue suit was velvet, and she believed the top was what people referred to as a smoking jacket. He wore cuff links and gold rings, one with blue stones. Sapphires, she thought. Clearly, he had plenty of money. "Did you get a good job?" she asked. "Is that how you got all the things you wanted?"

"I pursued my dreams." He studied her. "And I can tell you have dreams, too."

His soothing, understanding voice put Crystal at ease, and she nodded. "Yes, I do..."

One year later, Houston, Texas

The crowd yelled when Kyri walked onto the stage, but as she began playing her trademark riff, they went absolutely wild, roaring their approval and chanting her name again and again.

She launched straight into the hit which made her famous, soaring up the charts and reaching the Number One spot in record time. Her rich soprano rose and fell, sheer emotion reverberating through her voice. Her band blended in, backing her up as she dominated the stage. When it was time for her guitar solo, all the spotlights focused on her. Her fingers flew over the strings of her one-of-a-kind, specially made Les Paul, the notes accompanying her words perfectly. Reviewers were forever enthusing about her performances, saying she "blended pure magic with her voice and the genius of her guitar playing."

Time passed, with her and her band moving from one song to the next. At the end of the concert, her fans gave her one standing ovation after another.

"Kyri," a reporter called out later as she and the band left the auditorium, heading for their bus after the concert. "What do you attribute your monumental success to?" He added, voice pleading, "Will you say it for us? Please?"

"Satan, of course," she replied, laughing. Then she yelled, "All hail Sweet Satan!"

The clustered reporters and throngs of fans clapped and cheered.

During her first visit home after becoming famous, her parents had admitted to cringing when they'd heard her praising the devil. She'd explained her agent had told her she needed something to set her apart from other singers, and they'd acknowledged her desire to garner attention. As it turned out, the majority of her growing fan base interpreted her talk of Satan as a publicity stunt rather than her truly being a Satan-worshiper.

Keeping a smile pasted on her face, Kyri catered to the crowd, chatting with people, thanking them for their support, and stopping to sign autographs. One man wanted her to sign his arm in permanent marker, and she acquiesced, to his delight. But as soon as she and the others left their fans behind and boarded her oversize tour bus, her smile vanished.

She entered her private room, locking the door behind herself, and gently laid her guitar case on the bed. Opening it, she studied her Les Paul. This was her third but reminded her of how ecstatic she'd been to get her first. Sometimes she still couldn't believe how far she'd come since those days. Her eyes drifted over the initials C.J. inside the cover—for her birth name, Crystal Jernigan—and she took out the guitar, pressing her mouth to the bridge. She felt a stinging pain and winced, knowing she'd cut her lips on a sharp string.

The following morning

"Have you heard the news?" Rod, the band's lead drummer, asked.

"Huh?" Kyri yawned. "I haven't heard anything. I was exhausted last night after the concert, and I conked out fast."

"That's what we figured when you didn't come out of your room. We didn't want to bother you, especially with our tour schedule as packed as it is. We got you a meal for when you got hungry, though, and stuck it in the fridge."

"Thank you. I appreciate that. I'm starving. Hey, you mentioned something about the news? Don't tell me Tam added another unscheduled stop to our tour." Their agent, Tamarind, did that now and then, sometimes only telling them of changes at the last minute.

"The Slasher struck again."

Kyri said nothing but looked at him blankly.

"That's the serial killer who cuts people's throats and leaves them to bleed out," Rod said. "He's been at it for

10

more than a year."

"Yeah, I've heard of him."

"You'll never guess where he was last night."

"Where?"

"In San Antonio."

She frowned. "Are you serious or kidding around? I can't tell."

"It's true," bass guitarist Karl said, coming toward them. "The news stations are talking about it and pretty much nothing else. The killing happened right outside San Antonio, but we're not all that far from there."

Kyri bit her lip. "That's disturbing."

Three months later, Chicago, Illinois

A figure dressed in black walked down the dimly lit alley, staying in the darkest shadows.

Several feet behind, a man crept along and pulled a gun from his pocket. He lunged for the person in black, but found himself holding only a jacket, not his would-be victim. Cursing, he looked around, and something flashed in front of him. He tried to speak but gurgled instead, blood spurting from the fresh gash on his throat.

Once he'd crumpled to the ground, Kyri stepped forward and stooped by the dying man, careful not to step in the blood pooling around his head and shoulders. She opened her hand and studied the guitar string she held. It was made of the finest steel, and she carried it everywhere except for when it was strung on her guitar. She had from the beginning.

11

The blood staining the string only seconds before had already vanished. Knowing where it had gone, she felt a twinge of guilt, but only a twinge. It was nothing like the horror she'd experienced the first time she'd used it. She'd almost fainted that day and gotten sick to her stomach, vomiting repeatedly, and she'd had trouble eating and sleeping for weeks after. But each new use had been accompanied by increasing numbness.

Hearing faint voices in the distance, Kyri quickly laid the guitar string in the man's open wound. Doing so was part of the bargain she'd struck with the man she'd met in New Orleans.

She'd scoffed at first when he'd offered to make her dreams come true in any way she chose. In fact, she'd been sure he was nothing but a crackpot. But then he'd revealed his true form—that of a daemon. She'd been flabbergasted, but unable to ignore the evidence. Setting incredulity aside, she'd paid attention to his words. Although she'd shuddered at what was expected of her, he'd pointed out there were plenty of bad people in the world who deserved to die. That along with the thought of having everything she'd ever wanted—without effort or having to wait for it— had outweighed her reservations.

From the moment the daemon pricked her finger with the string, magically linking it to her, everything had fallen in place. Things would continue doing so, he'd said, as long as she upheld her end of their agreement.

The pool of blood beside Kyri shrunk slowly, and once it was gone, she recovered the string, put it in her pocket, and sped away. The magic revolving around her manifested in different ways depending on the circumstances, including the ability to travel long distances in a matter of minutes.

Her voice had changed, too. It had always been good, but had become truly amazing, no longer cracking, even on notes she couldn't reach before. Now she hit them with no effort at all. And her hands, insured by Lloyd's of London, danced across guitar strings, reaching extensions without strain. Ideas for new songs came to her often, each seeming better than the last, and all becoming hits. Overall, everything she did seemed to turn into sheer gold.

Five weeks later

"We love you so much," Mom said, spreading her arms.

Kyri rushed into them. "And I love you," she replied. She hugged Dad next, feeling secure and cherished in his arms, too. "I've missed you and being here feels wonderful." She meant every word. Staying busy with tours had prevented her from visiting for several months but being home brought back happy memories.

One thing bothered her deeply, though. If only she'd listened to Mom and Dad when... But she didn't want to dwell on negatives, especially ones she couldn't go back and change, and forced herself to concentrate on the moment.

They were sitting down to dinner when a tingling sensation spread throughout her body. She quivered, knowing what it meant. In recent weeks, more and more blood offerings had been demanded of her. In hopes of delaying the inevitable, she'd killed three people of her own volition the day before coming home.

As she glanced around the dinner table, terror welled up inside her, and she couldn't breathe. Her mother, father, and younger siblings were the only people in the home

13

with her, but she'd *never* hurt one of them. Never. Mumbling that her stomach hurt, she headed for a bathroom, but slipped out the back door instead. She ran for the woods half a mile away. After zipping through them, she arrived at her destination—a downtown park.

Kyri surveyed her surroundings, thinking at first that no one was around. But then she saw what she was looking for —a man seated on a bench by himself—and approached him.

Once she returned home, she eased into her kitchen chair and assured her parents the queasiness had passed, and she was fine. She could only manage a few bites of food, though.

She set her dirty plate in the sink after supper, and the tingling sensation started up again. When her mother walked by, chattering about all the things they'd do during her visit, Kyri felt actual nausea and threw up.

Clenching her jaws, she started to leave the room, but her feet moved against her will. Her chest tightened as she realized she was heading toward Mom. Struggling to draw air into her lungs, she fought to regain control of her body and make it do what she wanted. But her right hand moved toward her jean pocket. Horrified beyond belief, she knew the string must be there, despite her deliberately leaving it outside in her car.

Making jerky movements, she battled the magical demands and managed to force her feet into the hallway, up the stairs, and then into her bedroom.

She gasped, almost falling down, when the daemon appeared in front of her as a man. Fury twisted his handsome face into something horrific, and he morphed

14

into his satanic form fully. Flames blazed in his eyes and horns sprouted on his head.

"You defied me," he growled, the heat in his eyes blasting her. "Now pay the consequences."

She gagged at his sulfurous breath and felt as if her skin was on fire.

He bared his teeth and the guitar string appeared in the air in front of her. Before she could do anything, it slashed her throat, the sharp pain making her gasp. Blood squirted out of her neck, and she grabbed it with both hands, whimpering as she tried desperately to staunch the flow. She grew light-headed quickly, however, and collapsed on the floor, knowing she was dying.

But then she found herself standing up and touched her neck. The injury was gone.

"You get one chance," the daemon hissed, eyes boring into hers. "Only one. Next time I will rip you apart and yank out your soul. Now—*kill!*" He disappeared.

She stood there, shaking all over with tears streaming down her cheeks. The very thought of killing Mom and Dad was more than she could bear. Not to mention her little brother and sister, who were innocent and not to blame for any of this. What the daemon demanded was unthinkable, but...

Footsteps sounded from nearby. Stumbling from her room, Kyri saw her grandmother's back as the elderly woman entered the guest bedroom. She lived a few miles away but had apparently come for a visit.

Kyri's living nightmare was fresh in her mind. She relived her burning skin and her blood gushing out, the

15

coppery scent making her gag, the helpless feeling of not being able to do anything, and the sensation of her body landing on the cool floor. Trembling violently, she felt her legs wobbling underneath her and gulped in air, trying to breathe.

She felt something move and held out her right hand palm-up, watching the guitar string land there. Taking faltering steps down the hall, she took a deep breath and entered the room her grandmother was in, locking the door behind her.

 I Want to Be *Her*

NOT WANTING TO be caught staring, Elaiyne was careful to keep her eyes down, but she casually reached for her bottle of lemonade. She took a long, slow sip while glancing at the table to her right in the lunchroom, where Sonora sat beaming.

"It was the best day of my life," the other girl enthused, eyes sparkling. "Ever since my older sister started twirling, it's all I've wanted to do. I hoped I'd be chosen for the team, but I never dreamed they'd make me Head Majorette."

"I knew they would," Audrey replied. "None of the others are as good as you."

Friends sitting with them nodded. Classmates listening to the conversation from other tables did, too.

"You're saying that because you're my best friend." Sonora smiled at her warmly. "But thank you anyway."

"Hey, it's the truth. You're great at everything you do,

and you're a wonderful person, too." Most of the onlookers spoke up, agreeing.

A sense of wistfulness and desolation grew within Elaiyne as she listened, and she tightened her lips, trying not to cry. *"Why couldn't I have been born her instead of me?"* she wondered, despising everything about herself.

She'd give anything to be rid of her reddish-brown skin, which had the tendency to go blotchy and peel when she spent time in the sun. The Head Majorette's skin kept a peachy-golden hue year-round. Her curly, blonde hair was as stunning as a model's—in Elaiyne's opinion anyway—and nothing like her own, which was straight, black, and resisted her every effort to make it wavy. Her teeth weren't nice and straight like the other girl's, and her eyelashes were short nubs compared to the majorette's long ones. And her nose was too big, unlike Sonora's which was just right for her face. In fact, the only thing Elaiyne even half-way liked about herself were her blue eyes, but Sonora's green ones were a hundred times better. Shinier. Prettier. Her body was perfect, too—slender and curvy—unlike Elaiyne's. Her love for junk food reflected in her stomach, hips, and thighs being chubby, not to mention her upper arms which were slightly flabby.

She watched the other female take a bite of lettuce before announcing she was done and wished for the millionth time she was thinner. The majority of Sonora's meal lay untouched on her plate. She'd only eaten her salad and a piece of pear.

Elaiyne looked down at her own tray and sighed, frowning. She'd eaten every single bite.

18

That evening

"Honey, aren't you hungry?" Mom asked. "I prepared all your favorite foods tonight. Lasagna with extra cheese, garlic bread, baked potatoes loaded with butter, sour cream, cheese, bacon, and a bunch of other stuff. And I made cheesecake for dessert."

Elaiyne forced herself to smile. She hadn't heard her mother's footsteps in the hallway, or the door to her bedroom opening, but there Mom stood. "I'm still stuffed from lunch, but that sounds yummy."

"I'll put the leftovers in the fridge, and you can get some when you're ready."

"Thank you, Mom. You didn't have to make all that stuff, though. I know how tired you are after work."

"You're my child and I love you a great deal. You deserve nice things. And I wanted you to know I'm proud of you. I saw your new grades and you earned the highest GPA in your class again." Her mother walked over, leaning down to kiss the top of her head before hugging her. "You're brilliant. Funny. Great company. A total sweetheart, and the best daughter in the world."

Warmth suffused Elaiyne and she basked in the feeling of being cherished. "And you're the very best Mom." But then she thought about her appearance, wondered what in the world the older woman saw in her, and her happiness evaporated as if it had never been there.

A week later

"Why would you do this?" Mom asked, her face pale. "Bleach is strong. Caustic. It's not meant to go on our skin.

Whatever were you thinking?"

"I just wanted to make my skin lighter so it would look better," Elaiyne admitted. She wished her mother hadn't found out and bit her lip, trying not to wince as her mother gently washed her aching arms.

"But yours is *beautiful* as it is. I wish mine looked as healthy and tanned as yours does—did." A gasp escaped her daughter's lips and Mom stiffened. Her eyes dampened. "I'm so sorry, Honey. I'm trying to be careful and not hurt you, but that area is extra red and irritated."

"It's okay. I know you're just trying to get the bleach off."

Mom began applying antibiotic ointment. "I want your word you won't do this again."

Two days later

"I'm *fine*," Elaiyne insisted. "Really, Mom. I'm not hungry and I told you I was trying to lose some of my flab."

"But you have none. You've always been thin, but now your cheeks are getting hollow, and your arms look like toothpicks."

"No, they don't. They're still flabby."

Mom frowned; her eyes troubled. She shook her head slowly. "I don't know why you think that because it's not true. Our bodies need food to be strong and healthy; our minds, so they'll work their best. I don't know what's wrong, but I know something is... Come on. We're going to the doctor."

One week later

"You *promised*," Mom stressed, tears filling her eyes and escaping down her face. "Not putting bleach on your body applies to your head, too. Remember what I said about bleach? It's caustic. Your poor scalp... and your lovely hair..."

Elaiyne noticed the new shadows under the older woman's eyes and wondered if she'd put them there. She couldn't bear the anguish on her mother's face. "I'm sorry," she mumbled. "I just..."

"Don't you realize you're hurting yourself? Last time, you had red spots all over, but now you have wounds. We talked about this several times. The school counselor talked with you. Your doctor talked with you, but..." When Elaiyne turned away, saying nothing, Mom raised her voice. "Are you listening to me? This is important. Come here." She took her daughter's arm and steered her into the bathroom. "Take a good look."

Elaiyne raised her head and gasped at her reflection. She whirled to leave, but her mother carefully took her by the shoulders and turned her around.

"*I'm hideous!*" she wailed. Tears poured down her cheeks as sobs shook her body. "I look like a monster." Her hair was a ghastly shade of orangish-green, dry, and broken off in places, leaving the remainder different lengths. Patches were missing here and there on her head and lobster-red scalp shown through. The skin on her arms, shoulders, and upper chest which showed under her tank top was just as bad, scaly, and peeling. Even her eyes were bloodshot, because she'd accidentally gotten bleach in them while putting it on her hair.

21

Ten days later

Elaiyne tiptoed the whole way from her bedroom to the kitchen and opened the cupboard under the sink, freezing when it squeaked. Her heartbeat thundered in her ears like a runaway locomotive, and she expected her mother to come rushing in. Time passed without that occurring, and she finally relaxed. Grabbing what she'd come for, she returned to her room, locking the door behind herself.

She soon stared at her concoction, took an experimental sniff, and gagged. Even though she'd added lotion with aloe, the bleach smell was still overpowering, so she added more lotion. Her eyes stung—either from the bleach or paint thinner. A man on Facebook had said the latter would lighten skin, too, promising her it wasn't as harsh as bleach.

Remembering her return to school after the hair debacle, she shuddered. It had been dreadful, despite everyone being surprisingly nice. The wig Mom bought her had concealed the worst of the damage, but not the splotches on her face, neck, chest, and arms.

Sonora had been sympathetic, coming to tell her, "I'm sorry you were hurt. The people who goofed on that lotion should be ashamed of themselves. There are certain rules they're supposed to go by. Other people could've been hurt like you were. You could sue the company, you know."

Her kindness had made Elaiyne feel guilty for lying, but she couldn't very well reveal the truth. And, despite everything that happened, she longed to be the other girl more than ever.

She imagined herself as Sonora, being admired while she led the majorettes in a routine, being popular with all those friends. Looking like she did. A dreamy look and smile crossed Elaiyne's face, but she forced her mind back to reality.

Dropping a washcloth into her mixture, she prepared to spread the substance on herself.

The air shimmered, the floor unexpectedly vibrating under her feet. Across the room, something dark oozed out of the hardwood, not stopping until the shape was almost human-height, and Elaiyne forgot to breathe. Her mouth gaped when other shadows emerged, undulating back and forth, followed by a faint humming. She edged toward her door, but the way was blocked by dark blobs. Red eyes opened up in them, flickering eerily as they focused on her.

When she tried to yell for her mother, shadows shot across the room toward her. Something covered her mouth, and she found herself panting for air, unable to speak.

"You don't want to be you," a voice said, sounding as if it came from all around her. "But we do."

Something grabbed Elaiyne's right ankle, then her left, and she squealed and kicked, trying to get free. She failed. If anything, she felt the entities tighten their grip.

They began sinking into the floor, taking her with them. She screamed, but only for a second before something filled her mouth, preventing her from making a sound.

She twisted and struggled, trying to get away, but continued sinking farther and farther from sight. Other shadows blended together, coalescing into a large blob, then morphing into a vaguely human shape.

Within seconds, Elaiyne was gone, but they'd taken her place, duplicating her perfectly.

23

 ## Starting with a Drop

MOONLIGHT SHONE THROUGH the kitchen window, landing on the faucet, and making it gleam. A trace of moisture glistened at the end of the spout. As minutes passed, more accumulated, eventually falling with a faint *plip*.

The dripping increased and soon *plip*, *plip*, *plip* sounded. Within moments, a steady stream of sparkly, crystal clear water began to pour out, splashing as it fell into the basin. It began taking on a light yellow tinge which progressively deepened into a rich gold. The liquid thickened, becoming a gelatinous ooze which no longer produced any sound as it landed.

Instead of going down the drain, the substance accumulated in the sink, rising higher and higher. When the basin was almost full, the sludge abruptly stopped coming out of the faucet.

The old, rickety kitchen counter creaked, and the one-by-three-inch pieces of wood that held up the right side cracked. The pieces supporting the other side splintered before breaking completely, and the entire counter gave way, collapsing.

Ooze poured onto the floor from the sink and lay there glistening. The middle portion twitched ever-so-slightly. Doing so again, it then rose, moving this way and that. It gradually expanded, taking on a vaguely human shape. The upper part morphed into a woman with long, flowing blonde hair, but her lower portion elongated, changing into that of a snake.

Takudawa—a Naga—turned slowly, taking a good look around and studying her surroundings. She undulated across the kitchen on her tail, stopping by the stove and frowning at the unknown object. It was the first she'd ever seen. She tilted her head, stared at it, then poked it a few times with her finger. She did the same with the refrigerator, pushing it hard enough to make it rock back and forth.

Turning her back on the appliances, she focused on her reason for coming to the home in the first place—important enough to bring her from the sea. She entered the living room, scanning everything there. The walls were totally bare except for one thing, a picture of a grinning man who held up a fish. Stains and grime stood out on the couch and recliner, and a small bookshelf was coated with a thick layer of dust. Unwashed plates with leftover food littered the room, along with dirty clothes and shoes. Cigarette butts and beer cans filled a trash can next to the recliner, but more lay scattered around the floor, along with other discarded trash.

A piece of wadded paper lay on the floor beside the couch. It was partially flattened with dark smears on top as if someone had stepped on it with muddy footwear. The Naga bent to pick up the paper, smoothed out the creases, and studied the picture she held. Trees and a wide expanse of water complete with birds flying overhead had been drawn in a childish hand. Crayons had been used to color everything in bright shades, including the fish and birds, and all of them were smiling.

Takudawa set down the artwork and left the room, moving down the hallway. Stopping at the bottom of the staircase leading to the second floor, she looked up.

Mark's bed moved, the legs scraping against the floor. He mumbled something incomprehensible in his sleep and stretched, cracking his eyelids for only a second before shutting them again. Something stirred close by, but he wasn't aware of it. However, when his mattress squeaked, his eyes popped open.

A figure towered over him. He gasped, eyes widening, and opened his mouth to scream, but no sound came out.

"I saw you," the Naga hissed, her nostrils flaring as she stared down at him. She raised her tail in the air and slammed it down on him with enough force to crack his bones and make the legs of his bed break through the floor.

"*Help!*" Mark wailed. A jagged bone protruded from his side, blood seeping from the area, and he grimaced in pain. "*Monster!*" he cried. "Someone, *help me!*"

"There is only one monster here. *You!*" Takudawa backhanded him in the face.

He gagged and spat out blood and teeth. "Stop. *Please.*"

27

"Did you stop?"

Mark blinked once, then again, his eyes revealing incomprehension.

"I saw everything," the Naga accused. "You punished her for not helping her mother gather firewood, but she had already helped. When she was done, she started looking around for a pretty pebble. I ask you now—what was wrong with that? *Nothing!*"

His eyes narrowed through the tears. "I told her to quit playing around and get more wood. She should've minded."

"Why? You gathered none. You drank strong spirits while she and her mother did the work. She's little. You're full grown." Takudawa's voice lowered to barely a whisper. "Children are sweet and innocent, but you struck her as if she was a man your size. Several times."

"I'm her father," Mark spat. "And I have the right to discipline my child any time it's needed."

"What you did wasn't discipline. It wasn't right, and anybody who hurts a child deserves only one thing."

She beat him with her hands and tail, not stopping until every bone in his body was broken and he was well past unconscious.

After spitting on his motionless body, she slithered away, blood and numerous chunks of human flesh speckling her body. She glanced down at herself, and all traces of him vanished from her skin as if they'd never been there in the first place.

Takudawa eased open another door, studied the sleeping woman inside, and scowled. How a mother could produce a life, then fail to protect her child, was beyond the Naga's understanding. For a few moments, she considered ending another pathetic excuse for a parent, but decided not to. The female wasn't worth her time and energy.

The Naga located the girl, entered her room, and discovered she was sound asleep. She gently picked up the small body and studied the child's sweet little face before reaching out to heal the bruise on her cheek and the cracked bone in her skinny arm.

When Takudawa left the home, she wasn't alone. She took the girl with her.

 **Bad Manners**

"MOM!" **DYLORI YELLED.** "He did it again!"

"Tattletale," Gwondo accused, sticking his tongue out at her.

"Yeah, I'm telling—because of what you did. You're a horrible brother. The worst ever and I wish you hadn't been born."

Smirking, he ripped a branch off a nearby tree. Using it as a toothpick, he dug a reddish chunk of something from between his teeth and spat it onto the ground beside her feet.

"That's revolting." Dylori wrinkled up her nose. "Stinky, too." He just smiled. "What you did was wrong. I don't do stuff like that to you."

He shrugged. "Tasted good."

She glared at him, and turned to shout, *"Mom!"*

Thumps sounded in the distance, growing louder by the second, and the earth shook under their feet as their mother approached. The full-grown Pycarnisaurus Gigantus was hundreds of years old, at least twice the size of a Tyrannosaurus Rex, and towered over her children.

"What have you done this time, Gwondo?" she asked, deep voice rumbling.

"Why do you think I did something?" he countered. "Maybe Dylori was bad."

Mom merely stared at him.

He lowered his eyes and kicked the ground with his right front foot, sending dirt clods and clouds of dust into the air.

"Stop fidgeting," she said, but he ignored her.

"He ate Corba," Dylori reported, shooting him a nasty look. "That's my fourth boyfriend he's eaten."

"Is that true, Gwondo?" Mom asked. He shuffled his six feet and she sighed. "Son, we've talked about this before. Several times, in fact."

"But I was hungry," he whined.

"That's no excuse." Her voice was ice-cold. Stern. "I've taught you right and wrong, and about respecting others and having good manners. Now apologize to your sister."

He mumbled something inaudible.

"Gwondo!"

The young carnivore flinched. "Sorry," he muttered. "Next time I'll ask first."

Mom gently nuzzled the side of his head, and he leaned against her, shooting Dylori a triumphant glance.

"That's it?" she demanded, stomping a foot. "You're not going to punish him? He *ate* my boyfriend."

"You didn't care about Corba, and you know it," Gwondo claimed. "All you wanted him for was food."

"Yeah, for *me*," she retorted. "He was mine, not yours." She glared first at him, then at their mother.

"Your brother was in the wrong," Mom said, nuzzling her, too. "Gwondo, your cages are full. There was no reason for you to take from your sister. What you did was unfair and selfish. Now give your big sister one of yours."

His eyes widened. "But..."

"Not one of your catches," their mother clarified. "One of your *girlfriends*."

"I don't want to," he whined.

"If you don't give Dylori one, I'll give her *all* of them."

Gwondo's face fell, and he pouted. "She's always been your favorite."

"*Now!*" Mom bellowed, lowering her head until they were eye-to-eye. "And I don't mean later or another day."

"Oh, all right," he muttered, stomping away.

"Remember," she called after him. "We're a family, and there's no excuse for bad manners."

 Smoked

BETTIE FANNED THE air in front of her nose with her hand and winced. Although she looked like a sweet granny with her spectacles and fluffy white hair, she didn't wear her usual smile. Rodney, sitting one table over, was smoking and the fumes drifted her way again. He'd been several tables away when he first sat and lit up, but after she'd asked him to put more distance between them, he'd come closer instead. Bettie's chest felt tight — an unsurprising symptom of her COPD and asthma. "Rodney, could you please move farther away to smoke?"

As usual, he seemed oblivious to the trappings of common courtesy. Instead of answering her or doing as she asked, he yawned, stretched in slow motion, and stared out across the Pacific. In the distance, a buoy bobbed, and sunlight reflected off the ocean's choppy waves. Rodney looked at the large sign to the left which read "No Smoking. Oxygen In Use," smirked, and turned his back to Bettie.

Glancing at their coworker, Bill, who was making short work of a vanilla shake, Rodney pantomimed sticking a finger down his throat. Bill frowned and shook his head, but Rodney grinned and told Bettie, "Nobody said you had to sit here."

"My new tank was being delivered." She gestured to the oxygen strapped to the back of her wheelchair. "This is where I agreed to meet the deliveryman."

"Well, you got it, so why didn't you leave? Why stay to bug me?"

"Bug you? You weren't here then. *I* came out first. You came later and began smoking, although I've told you repeatedly that your smoking's hard on me."

"Tough!" He shrugged. "If you didn't like it, you should've moved. Like they say, suck it up, Buttercup." He took a long drag on his cigarette and blew smoke toward her.

"She told you she was here first, Rodney," Janie said. Unlike Bettie, she wasn't on oxygen, but she was a nonsmoker. "This side's nonsmoking and you know it. Lenny talked with you before."

The nursing home where they worked stood on a beautiful stretch of California coast. In order to capitalize on the ocean views, the home had two covered patios. One way off to the left was for smokers. The other to the right was for everyone else. Staff came out to relax, chat, eat, enjoy the breeze blowing in over the ocean, and occasionally feed the terns and gulls. Now and then they saw dolphins or whales in the distance. Patients walked outside or were wheeled there, including some using oxygen tanks.

Rodney screwed his face into a nasty grimace. "Waah, waah, Janie." Walking toward Bettie, he blew smoke into her face and flicked his cigarette butt onto the ground.

The smoke affected Bettie the way it always did; her chest tightened, and she coughed.

Strolling away, Rodney voiced a breezy, "Bye, Felicia."

—The Watchers' eyes blinked. They looked away. —

Janie patted Bettie's back, adopting a soothing tone. "Try to relax while I — ah, here we go! I've got your oxygen." She fit the tubing around Bettie's neck and helped position the nasal cannulas in her nostrils. "Breathe in, hon. This'll help. A good, deep breath. That's it. Good girl."

"Try to breathe nice and steady," Bill urged. "Focus on the sound of your breathing and think of something pleasant. Going fishing. The sound of waves lapping against the pier. Relaxing in the sun. You'll feel better pretty quickly."

Bettie soon reported, "The tightness eased up. Thank you, Janie. You, too, Bill."

"I say karma's real and Rodney's going to get it someday," Janie said to no one in particular. The other employees relaxing outside nodded.

"When karma does bite his butt," Bill said, "I hope it bites hard. Hey, break's over, folks."

Bettie reached for her wheels.

"Here," Janie offered. "Let me push instead of you fighting the wheelchair."

"Thank you." Bettie beamed. "You're a sweetheart." Her regular wheelchair had developed problems, and she'd been forced to revert to the old one in her garage. It was rusty and had to be hand maneuvered. Diminished upper-body and shoulder strength from a heart attack made it hard for Bettie to propel herself.

Janie spoke to Bettie after they'd gone inside the building. "Hon, you're sixty-seven compared to my thirty-eight. You should be home relaxing, not working or having to deal with the likes of that loser, Rodney." She raised a hand to forestall Bettie's reply. "I know, I know. You've told me what happened, but it's a shame you had to return to work."

"I enjoyed retirement and volunteering," Bettie admitted, "but someone had to take Mike." Her fourteen-year old grandson had lost his parents — including Bettie's only daughter Jean — in a head-on collision a few months ago. If Bettie hadn't stepped forward, Mike would've gone into foster care. Unfortunately, having another mouth to feed, especially a tall, husky teenager either going through a growth spurt or just perpetually hungry, meant she needed more money. He ate her out of house and home — literally. She'd been a stay-at-home mom, raising her and her deceased husband's children. Eventually she took a job as a clerk, where she'd made very little. Her resulting Social Security was meager, and she often had to choose what to pay. Rent or food? Food or medicine? Medicine or electricity? Now she had Mike's needs to consider, too.

So, she'd returned to work. Fortunately, she knew how to type and use computers, and she'd been ecstatic to be hired by the very place where she'd previously volunteered.

***

Three days later, while stopped at a traffic light, Rodney flicked his cigarette out his car window, ignoring the car beside him.

The other driver, an elderly man, had his windows down and jumped when the smoldering missile flew into his vehicle and landed between his legs. With a yell, he squirmed and managed to grab it. "Don't throw cigarettes in folks' cars!" he fussed at Rodney.

Answering with a one-finger-salute, Rodney lit another cigarette. As soon as the red light turned green, he deliberately sent the cigarette flying at the other driver. "Waah, waah, waah," he taunted, zooming away.

The elderly man must have accidentally taken his foot off his brake, because his car rolled and drifted into another lane. Other drivers saw his head vanish. "Put it in park!" someone yelled. The old man's head popped up and his car halted abruptly.

A woman pulled alongside him. "Are you okay, sir? I'll call 911 and report that jerk."

He tossed something out his window. "He threw a cigarette into my car. I'm glad I found it, but now there's a burn hole in my seat." Then he shrugged. "Don't bother calling the police, dear. I didn't get that rude fellow's license plate or even the make of his car."

"I didn't, either" she admitted. "Well, are you good or do you need help?"

"I'm good. Thank you kindly for your kindness, ma'am."

39

—The Watchers did not look away. —

Forty minutes later, another man honked and yelled after Rodney, who'd sped past him, "Slow down, idiot! You're not supposed to drive like that in a school zone!"

Rodney snorted and pushed on the gas. Why should he care about some stupid kids? They probably had *real* parents who spoiled them, unlike him. His parents had abandoned him when he was little. He'd been in foster care for years before being adopted and deserved some of life's perks for being dumped. After all the time he'd waited, those perks were yet to come. How fair was that? Everyone got what they wanted *except* him!

He remembered visiting his foster-turned-adoptive mother last week. She'd turned him down flat when he'd asked for a new car, saying she couldn't afford it. He knew better. She had foster kids in her home, and that meant she got state money every month. She could've helped him if she'd wanted to. She was like everyone else, unwilling to help a deserving guy out!

Bitterness flooded Rodney and he ground his teeth together. He ignored the red stop sign on the bus stopped twenty yards ahead to his right and pushed down hard on his gas pedal. His car leaped forward, almost striking the children crossing in front of him. Laughing, he sped on after the bus driver yelled, "Watch out for the kids!"

—The Watchers' eyes were cold. —

***

Driving to work late two days later, Rodney swerved from the left lane into the right with no warning, almost side-swiping the vehicle there. The woman, who was driving a van full of children, jerked her wheel hard to the right to avoid being struck. The road was slick with rain, and she fish-tailed into a ditch, missing an electric pole by inches.

Rodney heard crying and screams behind him but kept driving. "Whiny brats." He didn't give them another thought.

—The Watchers' eyes narrowed, looking at one another in unspoken agreement. —

***

Four hours later, several employees, including Bettie and Janie, sat outside the nursing home, eating, and sharing pictures of grandchildren and pets. One man spoke of his plan to take his grandkids fishing during the upcoming weekend, and how excited the kids would be to ride in a boat for the first time. Another staff member broke a piece of bread into pieces and tossed them onto the ground nearby. Gulls dived to snatch them up. A couple of them landed and walked toward the people. Janie threw the birds some of her French fries, which were rapidly devoured.

"Man, stop being a douche," Bill griped at Rodney, who was smoking. "You know you shouldn't smoke right here. Some people can't handle it."

41

"So what?" Rodney shrugged. "If they don't like it, they can move." Everyone either grimaced, glanced at each other knowingly, or ignored him altogether. His eyes narrowed. How dare they whine over stupid kiddie and animal pictures but dismiss him? He'd show them, especially that insipid Bettie who'd taken his job. He'd applied for it first but took an orderly position when she stole the one he'd wanted. The fact that he lacked typing and computer skills didn't concern him.

Noticing a few inches of Bettie's oxygen line lying slack on the ground, he moved near, then positioned a foot beside it. No one noticed, and he eased his foot on top, bearing down with all his weight. Leaning close to a woman — ostensibly to study her Dachshund photo — he twisted his foot right and left on the line. Lighting a cigarette, he blew smoke at Bettie, despite coworkers berating him.

She had trouble breathing within moments, and this time her oxygen didn't help.

Rodney left amidst clamoring voices. Would she drop dead and free up his job? He didn't see Janie locate the crushed hose or Bill run for a replacement.

—The Watchers' eyes blazed. —

An hour later Rodney smoked in the nonsmoking area once more, although he'd already used up his breaks. He scowled over his failed sabotage and intended to try again.

He took a hard draw on his cigarette, and it twitched in his fingers. Blinking, he wrote that off as a trick of the light.

Then it moved again, and he froze. His mouth fell open when the cigarette got bigger, and he dropped it. This had to be a trick — those dopes inside getting back at him. But how could they make a cigarette expand?

It kept growing — to three feet in length and as big around as a small dog. "I'll be rich when the tabloids hear about this," Rodney gloated aloud. His eyes widened as the cigarette bent in the middle and rose like a person standing. Two eyes stared from the top portion — was that the head?

The cigarette-person-thing soon topped six feet, taller and huskier than Rodney. Bending over him, it whispered, "I'm from the world of Karma's Watching, and I came here for *you*." Its eyes glowed an eerie green.

Rodney froze. *That can't be good*, he thought. He shot up to run away, but the being seized him as if he weighed nothing and flipped him sideways, holding him like a spear. The whimpering man stopped moving and shrank into a cigarette almost instantly.

Meanwhile, Mr. Cigarette was taking Rodney's shape.

Human Rodney would've yelled but couldn't speak. Cigarette Rodney flicked a lighter, lit the former-man's feet on fire, then sucked on the filter, which had previously been the old Rodney's head.

Feeling searing heat in his feet, Old Rodney tried to scream but couldn't. His mouth was full of tobacco.

Cigarette Rodney drew hard on the filter and Old Rodney felt his feet withering. The physical pain faded into a numb pressure, but the panicked terror and emotional pain of knowing what was happening was excruciating. His calves burned away quickly — next, his thighs — then his hips. Old Rodney wailed soundlessly but could do nothing.

43

Horror filled him as his stomach burned up and the smolder moved up his chest.

Within seconds, Old Rodney's cigarette body was gone. Only fragments of consciousness remained, encapsulated in the filter.

Studying that very filter, New Rodney tossed it onto the ground. He positioned his right foot over it and bore down with all his weight, swiveled his foot back and forth, and ground what was left into smithereens.

New Rodney stretched, inhaled the fresh air, and enjoyed the breeze blowing on him. Looking at the ocean, he watched a dolphin leap out of the water and go back under as gulls flew overhead. Then he sauntered toward the nursing home doors. It wouldn't do to be fired his first day on the job. As bits of paper, tobacco and ash blew away behind him, he smiled and said, "Bye, Felicia."

 ## Deep in the Swamp

DAMPNESS HUNG IN the air, heavy as a wet blanket, and tendrils of fog crept over the water in the swamp, soon moving across the nearby shore. The usual cacophony of noise rang out from all directions, insect chirrs competing with bird calls, along with the deeper, basso coughs of bullfrogs and other animal sounds.

A rat emerged from a cluster of brambles and froze, whiskers twitching. It looked one way, then another, before scampering several yards to its right, stopping to drink water which had gathered in a small depression in the mud.

Without any warning, an enormous crocodile exploded out of the swamp, lunging for the smaller animal, which barely managed a startled squeak before being devoured.

***

Wahasi's stomach growled as she stalked away, grinding her teeth together. Her catch had been nothing but a morsel, doing little to assuage her hunger. Infuriated beyond belief, she raked the ground with her claws, leaving deep furrows. Rage boiled through her, quickening her steps. To think that she was reduced to *this*. In her hundreds of years, she'd never once stooped to eating common vermin. Not until today. This was intolerable, and she would never endure it again.

Kula would've understood her anger. No doubt he would've felt the same. But he was gone. Even his mastery of hoodoo, witchcraft, and the black arts hadn't been enough to prolong his life beyond a certain point.

The night they'd met for the first time, she'd attacked him, and he'd barely escaped with his life. She'd raged at the sorcerer's temerity, treating her as if she were a being he could command, when she was anything but. Although she hadn't been well-known, in one of her past lives she'd been an attendant to Sokol, an ancient Egyptian god, and she'd shared some of his abilities. She'd been reborn a queen, and in her latest existence, she'd found herself wearing the skin of a cocodrie—a crocodile—and taken a liking to the form. In fact, it was her favorite out of all of them.

She'd retained certain powers, even as a crocodile, so returning to the underworld after the summoning would have been quite easy. But she hadn't existed as long as she had by being stupid, and she'd studied the modern world closely. It had intrigued her on many levels. So had Kula, and his knowledge of magic had also been a potent lure.

He'd recognized how advantageous a partnership between them could be before she had and made a point of treating her with the utmost respect. Recognizing her

46

interest in his magic, he'd begun sharing morsels of it with her. In return, she'd revealed tidbits of her own and eventually loaned him strength.

They'd accepted one another as full collaborators over time, even becoming friends, sharing a common dislike of people. Kula's was a deep-seated hatred, a burning resentment he'd carried inside since he'd been labeled "crazy" by the Louisiana bayou people he'd grown up around. They'd criticized him for delving into the dark arts and punished him for doing so, ultimately ostracizing him. He'd taken refuge in the deepest, darkest swamp he could find. Wahasi had no personal grudge against humans but considered them a pest. One thing she and Kula had agreed on was their utter uselessness in every way but one.

Remembering how well she and the sorcerer had worked together, along with their unrealized goals, she snarled, slamming her paws down with each step. But dwelling on the past changed nothing, irritating her, so she redirected her focus. She much preferred to envision her future. To have one, though, she needed more than the occasional vermin, frogs, birds, or the like. She needed food —real food—before she weakened further and lost her abilities.

Even though she'd sworn an oath to Kula, Wahasi knew she had to break it. She had no choice if she was to survive, and that was more important than anything else right now.

She picked up speed and smashed through the sorcerer's cabin door, heading for the cabinet which contained his most prized possessions and strongest spells. Made of centuries-old hawthorn, it had been spelled for invisibility and to keep people out, but that didn't limit her in any way. In fact, not so long ago, she herself had added one important item to the cabinet—Kula's heart. In accordance with his wishes, she'd ripped it from his body after his death.

Several hours later

Wahasi thrashed on the ground, bellowing in defiance and exasperation. Kula's essence, which had been magically sealed in his heart, had been released after she'd eaten it, and he fought her now, raging about what she'd done.

"I *trusted* you!" he screamed in her mind, his energy surging throughout her body in all directions at the same time.

Rocked by his internal blasts, she felt as if she'd explode. *"Listen!"* she roared. "I had no choice."

But she understood why he felt betrayed. Their plan had been for her to find an appropriate, replacement body for his heart so he could live again.

Four days later

Wahasi's eyes popped open. She hadn't slept in longer than she could remember, but the battle waged inside her had drained her energy. However, it had finally ceased once an exhausted Kula had stopped fighting, listened to her explanation, and accepted her actions.

Realizing she lay on her back, with half her body submerged in water, she flipped over and dove into the swamp. A new energy coursed through her. She surged this way and that, luxuriating in the feel of liquid rushing past her, water churning as she rolled and propelled herself along.

Kula's magic bubbled inside her stomach, tickling, and intriguing her before expanding. Her mind filled with ideas, possibilities, and new knowledge.

As she emerged from the water, she shed her crocodile skin, taking a different form. Setting one foot on land, then the other, she studied them, her breath catching in her throat as she marveled at how dainty they were.

Wahasi tilted her head back, closing her eyes and taking a deep breath. Swamp scents, different in her changed form, yet still familiar, bombarded her nostrils, making her gasp in sheer pleasure. A humid breeze kissed her now-human, naked skin, and she shivered, watching sweat bead on it. She couldn't wait to try out this body and wondered what she could do with it.

Tingling slowly spread through her, goosebumps pebbling all over her.

"Anything," Kula whispered in her mind. "We can do *anything.*"

Their consciousnesses melded, and they were of one accord as to their next step.

As Waha-Kula strode through the swamp, they gestured toward the water. Streams of liquid rose into the air. Soaring toward them, the liquid encased their body, solidifying into a dark-green gossamer gown. They pointed at a nearby bush loaded down with reddish-purple berries. Dozens flew through the air, covering their feet and changing into high-heeled boots.

***

One after another, the bar's patrons turned to stare at the

woman who'd entered. Jet-black hair streamed down her back. She had a heart-shaped face with lush, red lips, skin a shade between ivory and cream, and eyes a startling shade of green. Although she was clothed strangely given the setting—a strapless, floor-length gown that melded to her body like a second skin, and purplish-red, high-heeled boots—the attire seemed fitting.

"Her face is to die for," a woman whispered to her boyfriend. "Her body, too." Both of them stared wide-eyed at the beauty.

Men and woman alike were captivated, finding themselves unable to look away. When the stranger spoke, invisible tendrils of magic floated from her lips, lightly caressing each watcher's face before wrapping tightly around them and sinking into their bodies.

When Waha-Kula changed into a crocodile, the people said and did nothing, their eyes staring forward blankly. They remained silent, enchanted, even as the cocodrie-sorcerer began savagely ripping chunks of flesh from the closest individual. After devouring their fill, Waha-Kula morphed back into a woman, and all signs of the feeding vanished.

They made their way to the next establishment, then the next, their silent followers trailing behind them. By the time Waha-Kula left town, dozens of people followed them.

Their gown and boots vanished as they reached the swamp, wading deep into it. The smells they knew so well filled their nose, washing over and around them. The humid air encased their body in moisture, and they smiled. Clothing their body in cocodrie skin once more, they dove into the swamp, losing themselves in the sensation, then

50

rolled in the mud, enjoying that just as much as the swimming.

"Please," Kula beseeched later, voice breaking. "This is pleasurable, but I've waited so long..."

Wahasi agreed without speaking and took control of their body. She changed into a human again and raised her arms into the air, invoking the most powerful magic she knew, blending Kula's power with her own.

Looking at her right hand, she changed one finger into a jagged crocodile claw, and used it to cut a deep gash between her breasts, going straight through the bone. Her chest opened wide, and she reached inside, slicing off a portion of her heart before allowing her body to heal itself.

She held the piece she'd removed in her cupped palms and concentrated, narrowing her eyes. Tiny particles of flesh flew from her body toward her hands. Similar fragments drifted to her from the mesmerized people.

The portion of heart grew larger and larger until the task was complete. Wahasi then studied the individuals who'd followed her from town, focusing on a tall, dark-haired man who bore a strong resemblance to Kula. She beckoned him forward, slashed open his chest, and replaced his heart with the one she'd grown.

The man gasped and his eyes widened, changing from their original brown to a bright blue Wahasi knew well.

Kula yelled exultantly. "I'm back," he announced, grabbing Wahasi for a tight hug.

"*We're* back," she replied, eyes sparkling. Gesturing at the townsfolk surrounding them, she laughed. "Are you ready for a feast?"

51

His form flickered, grew hazy around the edges, and he transformed into a huge crocodile. "I *love* your power," he growled, teeth bared into a ferocious grin. "I could get used to this."

Wahasi changed into a cocodrie, too, her eyes meeting his in unspoken agreement.

They whirled at the same time, charging toward the closest people.

 **The Brat**

"BRAD, STOP THROWING food," Ginger told her twelve-year-old son.

Acting as if she hadn't even spoken, Brad flung a chunk of cantaloupe at his sister, Eva, who was six. It struck the side of her head, making her wail. Ginger hurried to remove the remaining fruit from the kitchen table and gently cupped Eva's cheek, managing to soothe her cries.

"You're going into timeout if you don't stop, Brad."

His face darkened ominously as he glared at her. Grabbing a handful of scrambled eggs, he slung them in her direction. They hit her forehead and glasses, tumbling down her new blouse. Gleefully laughing, he slung some at Eva, who began to cry once more.

Tensing up, Ginger took a deep breath, fighting the urge to cry or scream. The day had barely begun, and Brad was already...

She and her husband had adopted him four years earlier. He'd been a handful from the very start, continued to be one even at the best of times, and showed no signs of stopping or behaving anytime soon. When he'd been kicked out of every school in town, they'd uprooted their family from southern Texas, moving from one city to the next, finally arriving in the northwest portion of the state. They'd taken Brad to numerous doctors, psychologists, and psychiatrists, who'd mentioned possible diagnoses of ADHD and ODD, and even tried medication, but his behavior had remained the same. The experts' overall consensus had been "behavior problems," along with early signs of sociopathic tendencies.

Brad shot Eva a nasty look before nabbing a fork. Ginger hurried to take it. She snatched away the spoon he grabbed, too. There was no telling what he planned to do with utensils but given his history of hitting people with anything he could get his hands on, Ginger had no doubt it would be bad. He certainly didn't need a fork or spoon for eating because he had no food left. He'd already thrown it everywhere.

Brad grabbed the butter knife from beside Ginger's place and stabbed the table.

She asked for it, but he ignored her. Her eyes widened, darting from him to Eva when she realized he was glaring at his sister. A pit opened in Ginger's stomach when he moved toward the six-year-old, and she grabbed his hand, trying to pry the knife from his hands. He kicked her over and over.

She wrapped her arms around him, keeping a hand firmly on the knife while trying to restrain him, but he struggled to get free.

54

Experts had taught her and her husband the best way to restrain but being forced to do it was frustrating. In fact, Ginger felt nothing *but* frustration and wondered how long she could keep this up. Brad had been known to act out for hours before. He usually wouldn't cooperate, no matter what, and seldom showed remorse, regardless of what he'd done, who he'd hurt, or what he'd demolished.

"Art, can you come here?" Ginger called to her husband who'd been showering as she'd left their bedroom earlier.

"What's up, Hon?" he replied, his feet thumping as he hurried down the stairs.

No explanation was needed when he entered the kitchen, and he immediately hurried to take over with their son.

"Stop," Art admonished after Brad yanked an arm free, and struck his father. Art secured the arm, glanced around, and winced. "The food everywhere?"

Ginger nodded, her shoulders drooping. She felt completely demoralized. The kitchen looked as if a tornado had swept through, even though she'd cleaned up earlier before the kids woke up. She'd have to redo everything.

Eva sniffled. Her Halloween costume, chosen just for the contest at school today, bore evidence of Brad's misbehavior.

Sighing, Ginger knew her daughter would have to change into her old costume and hoped that wouldn't prompt another round of tears. She remembered the flying eggs and examined herself, discovering stains on her blouse. She'd be late getting the kids to school and herself to work, even though she'd gotten up extra early. After all, she couldn't show up with dirty clothing and bits of egg in her

55

hair.

***

That evening, Bradley sulked at the dinner table, refusing to eat or talk.

Ginger and Art exchanged a meaningful glance, silently agreeing that this was better than an outburst.

Although they tried not to use physical punishment, they didn't regret spanking him earlier. He'd run amok at school, refusing to mind, listen, or do anything he'd been told. He'd kicked classmates and his teacher, damaged other children's Halloween costumes, and acted overall as if his only interest lay in harassing everyone. As a result, the principal had suspended him for three days.

His parents had originally planned to ground him from his TV and video games, along with assigning him extra chores, but still let him go trick-or-treating. However, they'd changed their minds after picking him up. Not only was he unrepentant about his behavior at school, but he'd picked on Eva on the way home, tearing up her homework and marking on her costume with a pen.

"I *hate* you," Brad yelled at Ginger, throwing his plate onto the floor, sending ceramic shards and food everywhere before turning to Art. "I hate you, too! You're mean."

He ran from the table, and up the stairs, presumably to his room.

"He hates me, too," Eva whispered.

"No, he doesn't," Art reassured her. "I'm sure he doesn't hate any of us. He's just upset because he got in trouble and can't go trick-or-treating."

"Jana says he's *bad,*" Eva shared about her best friend. "She said her father would've torn up his butt if he was their family."

***

Three hours later, Brad crept from his room, pausing in the hallway outside his door to listen. He peered into his parents' and sister's rooms, finding them sound asleep. In the kitchen, he helped himself to some cold meat loaf and one of the three remaining pieces of pie from the refrigerator. Two were saran-wrapped, one labeled "Mr. Witenour," the other "James." Brad had no idea who those people were, but didn't care anyway, and ate those pieces as well. He spotted his sister's Halloween bucket, crammed some of her candy into his mouth, poured the rest onto the floor, and crushed it with his feet.

He glared at his sister's artwork on the fridge, tore it into several pieces, and shoved it into the garbage, pushing it underneath other things. Coffee grounds and cantaloupe seeds got on his hands, but he wiped them on the curtains. Realizing his parents would see the candy fragments still lying on the carpet, he gathered them up, flushing all of them down the toilet.

No one was around to bother him, so he took his time circling the living room. Eva's latest school photo was on the wall next to his. Snatching hers down, he slung it out the back door, followed by the plaque his mother had just been awarded at work.

"They'll see them," he muttered, going to retrieve them. He stomped on the two items before hiding the pieces in a neighbor's trash can.

Brad returned to his bedroom, dozing off soon after lying down. But he woke thinking he'd heard something. He listened, but nothing caught his attention, so he closed his eyes.

Scratch, scratch.

Hearing the faint sound, he sat up in bed.

Scratch, scratch, scratch.

It came from the far side of his room. Tiptoeing over, he pressed his ear to the wall, and heard more scratching. Mice must've gotten inside again. Dad put traps throughout their home last time, catching several little intruders.

A scurrying sound came from behind him, and he whirled, not seeing anything. It had to be mice.

Tapping over his head made him flinch, and he stared at the ceiling.

"Man, those things are really moving," he murmured. Shrugging, he lay down, this time positioning earbuds in his ears so he'd only hear music.

Red eyes stared into Brad's, and he gasped. Throwing off his covers, he jumped out of bed. His heart thumped as if it was trying to escape his chest, and he felt light-headed. The floorboards were cold under his feet, and that's when he realized he'd been asleep. He didn't hear anything and felt foolish. Of *course*, nothing was in his room. Even so, he turned on the TV, putting the sound low enough not to keep him up but high enough to drown out any other mouse or night sounds. He fell asleep almost as soon as his cheek hit his pillow.

He dreamed something brushed his nose, making it itch. Then something touched his neck, and squeezed his throat, slowly tightening its grip until he had trouble breathing. He woke gasping for air, felt his throat with his hands, but nothing was there.

Rustle, rustle, click, click came from behind him.

"Stupid mice," he muttered, turning around even though he knew the darn things wouldn't be in plain sight.

Eyes widening, he almost fell over his own feet backing away.

A hand was on the floor in front of him, not attached to anything. Brad stared open-mouthed, jumping when the fingers wiggled, then started to pull themselves in his direction. *Click, click, click.* The sound came from the long, badly chipped fingernails hitting the floor.

The strange thing was covered in thick hair, the fingers slightly bent, resembling a spider's legs as they advanced toward the boy.

He took a step back, eyeing the door across the room.

With no warning, the hand jumped into the air, flying toward him with fingers widespread.

Brad screeched, fell over backwards, landing on the floor beside his bed. He immediately noticed movement in the darkness underneath.

A second hand crawled into view. He scrambled to his feet, racing for the door, but another hand dropped from the ceiling, blocking his path. More hands emerged from his closet.

A grotesque face with eerie green eyes and a misshapen, elongated mouth appeared on one hand, then on another. Soon, they all had faces.

Whispers sounded from around Brad before the creatures started toward him. Hands ran across the floor on their fingertips. Some traveled through the air.

He wildly swung his arms, kicking and fighting to get the things off his body, but more appeared.

The hands pushed him to the ground, ignoring his screams and thrashes while pulling him toward his bed. A final wail tore from his mouth as they drug him underneath, into the darkness.

 **Witches Aren't Real**

THE WITCH SWOOPED to the right on her broom, darted left, then rocketed straight upward, her robe flapping in the wind.

Six-year-old LaShelle giggled, eyes sparkling as she watched from the ground below. But when the figure above her abruptly jerked, hurtled downward, and crashed into the branches of a tree, she burst into tears.

"Don't cry, sweetie," Mama soothed. "I'm sure your kite's fine. It'll be easy to get down." She shifted the sleeping baby in her arms before turning to her thirteen-year-old son. "Devin, will you go up and get it, please?"

Engrossed in a game on his phone, he didn't reply.

"*I want my kite!*" LaShelle wailed, stomping her feet.

"Heck!" Devin looked up from his cell, glaring at his little sister. "I lost because of you and your stupid whining. All you do is whine about crashing that ugly kite."

"My kite isn't ugly," she retorted, her bottom lip trembling. "It's *beautiful!*"

"It's a nasty, old witch," he taunted. "Witches are stupid. They aren't even real."

"Stop being mean," Mom interjected, frowning at him. "Her kite is just as nice as yours, and she didn't crash it on purpose. You know how gusty the wind has been."

Devin snorted, but climbed the tree, recovering the witch in a matter of minutes. "She'll just going to get it stuck again," he complained, after LaShelle skipped away with her kite. "It should've been mine anyway, not hers. I asked for it first."

"Yes, you did, but you decided to get the dragon instead, remember? I know you're upset it broke, but that's not your sister's fault. Yours can be fixed. We just need some materials from the store."

Three hours later

Devin grinned after beating another level on his game, but his eyes widened when he realized the sky was darkening. He'd completely lost track of time. Mom had given him permission to stay in the park when she and the rest of the family left, but he was supposed to have been back by now. Knowing he was in trouble—*big* trouble—he hurried down the road toward home.

A dog barked in the distance, but he ignored it, breaking into a run. But when he heard a cracking noise from nearby, he nearly stumbled and froze, looking around. It sounded as if someone had stepped on a stick, and he wondered if one of his friends who lived in the area was trying to scare him.

"I know you're there," he called. "Come on out."

Cackling laughter rang out from all around him. He heard a whooshing sound and looked up to see a witch flying toward him on a broomstick.

Devin snickered at first, but got a better look, and his mouth fell open. "Y—you're not a kite!" he exclaimed, backing away.

"No, I'm not," the witch crowed. "I'm quite real. And you're perfect!" She grabbed him by his arm, tossed him over her broom, and zoomed away.

 **Aokigahara Forest**

"LET'S LEAVE." SHARYN'S voice was barely audible. *"Please."*

"Why are you whispering, Babe?" Abner asked. "No one else is here, just us."

"Because of where we are," she replied, speaking even softer than before. "I have the strangest feeling someone's watching us. Don't you feel it?"

"Of course not." He rolled his eyes. "That's ridiculous."

"No, it isn't. My skin is crawling. There's got to be a reason for that."

"Hon, I love you something fierce, and you mean the world to me, but sometimes you're such a little girl."

A faint tapping sound came from nearby, and she took a sharp breath, eyes widening. "You must've heard that, right? You're wrong about us being alone. Something's out there."

Abner snorted. "Well, d'uh. Of course, there is. We're in a forest. It's probably a woodpecker."

"I doubt any are here. At home in Texas, yes, but we're in Japan." When he didn't reply, Sharyn pressed. "This whole place gives me the heebie jeebies. We should go before something bad happens."

"Like what? A mosquito biting your butt? Where's your sense of adventure?"

"Dead and gone, at least since you started hounding me to accompany you. This forest has a really bad reputation because of the deaths that occurred here, and I don't think we should've come."

He touched her cheek gently. "Don't work yourself up needlessly. I'm fine. You're fine and have nothing to worry about. I promise you that."

"I know you're trying to reassure me, but…"

"Babe, I saw the same things you did about this place, and they were *fascinating*. That's why I wanted to visit. Everyone says it's one of the most haunted places in Japan. People have seen and heard all sorts of stuff. Hopefully, we will, too." Abner's eyes flashed, and he held up his new camera. "I really want to catch something with this."

"There were *lots* of deaths. People killed themselves." Sharyn chewed her thumbnail. "Locals call it Suicide Forest, and that doesn't appeal to me, especially since you insisted on coming now instead of earlier."

"What's wrong with now?"

"It's nighttime. Dark."

66

"The darkness makes being here even better."

"For you, maybe, but I don't *want* to see anything other-worldly, Abner. I don't want to be scared. I'd much rather be back in our hotel room with that great mini-bar and jacuzzi."

"Do you really want to tell everyone at home you traveled all the way to Japan, but didn't visit the most famous sites? That you chose to just sit in a hotel instead?"

She didn't answer, but bit her lip, and glanced around once more.

"Look at you." Abner snickered. "You're all pale and jumpy."

"I mean it. We should go back."

Paying no attention to her words, he strode forward, and Sharyn had to hurry to catch up.

"Look, Hon." He pointed at a tree to their right. "The branches on that one are bent at strange angles. It almost looks like…"

She shrieked when something cold brushed against her neck. "*Something touched me!*"

"I felt it, too. But it's nothing. Just a breeze."

However, he took an involuntary step backward when a Japanese man and woman stepped out of the shadows directly to the right of them.

"Hello," Sharyn said, smiling at the two. "You sure were quiet. I didn't hear you coming."

"Join us," the other woman said in a monotone. She spread her arms as if offering a hug.

"I think we're all right on our own," Abner replied, his

voice cool. When the newcomers didn't move, he spoke again. "Never mind. We'll just go." But he gasped, face paling, when the two strangers vanished, reappearing only feet in front of him and his wife.

The other man reached up, plucked a scythe from the air, and swung it, missing Sharyn's body by mere inches.

She shrieked. Abner grabbed her by the arm, shoved her behind him, and snatched a branch off the ground. He swung it at the attacker, but it passed right through him.

Sharyn whimpered, hastily backing away, and almost falling over a small bush behind her.

But she and Abner exchanged worried glances when more individuals appeared around them. Men, women. Old, young. It was clear they were all apparitions since the woods could be seen right through their bodies. One man holding a ghostly handgun had blood running down his face from a hole in his temple. A sword protruded from another's stomach. Blood poured from an open gash in one woman's throat, but a second clutched bottles of pills, then held them out to the American visitors.

"Join us," she whispered.

The others spoke in unison, repeating those same words again and again, their volume increasing until it was shattering in intensity.

Whimpering and moaning, Abner and Sharyn clamped their hands over their now-bleeding ears.

***

"Aokigahara Forest's Death Toll Rises" was the headline of a local newspaper the following day. In the article, reporters summarized the history of "Suicide Forest" before focusing on the most recent deaths—those of an American couple who'd told family and friends they were visiting Japan to celebrate their first anniversary. Authorities wondered if there was more to the story.

 Aziza

AZIZA TREMBLED, HER legs wobbling and almost giving way beneath her.

Heart beating faster, the thirteen-year-old became a bit light-headed,

tried to breathe slowly but couldn't. She willed herself to be calmer,

but it didn't work, her chest tightening. Biting the inside of her cheek—

hard—she tasted blood, swallowed without thinking, and hoped the

discomfort would help her focus and bring her the calm she did seek.

It didn't. She bit herself again, eyes dampening, but not from the pain.

Remembering the past, her resentment grew, taking on a

life of its own.

She tried to push the bad memories aside, but they surfaced once again.

Murmuring voices rose and fell around Aziza, nobody paying attention

to her or even glancing her way. Some people in the crowd were talking

louder now, others shouting; several latecomers approached on the run.

Her own feelings intensified, face warming up first, then her entire body,

sweat beading on her skin. The queasiness in the pit of her belly grew,

burning intense and hot, soon a maelstrom churning out of control. She

wondered if she'd explode or turn into pure flame. Hands tingling a bit

and slick with sweat, she wiped them on her tunic, but the sensations

didn't stop. One palm shimmered faintly, a tiny flame popping out of it.

She shut her hand, releasing the breath she hadn't known she was holding,

and darted a quick look at the townsfolk. For all the attention they paid her,

she could've been dirt. Their eyes never wavered from the

scene unfolding

in the center of the village. Some of them bent to the rock-covered ground,

picked up handfuls, then drew back their raised arms to throw the stones.

A woman cried out, and Aziza flinched. Studying the individuals around

her, she saw nothing but sheer condemnation on their faces, and tightened

her lips. Marda didn't deserve this. She'd been nothing but good, using her

vast knowledge of herbs to help and heal, and many lives she'd brightened.

Aziza alternated between sweating and having chills, nobody noticing when

she slipped away, heading straight into the woods so people wouldn't see her.

Closing her eyes, she thought of her childhood, remembering way back then.

Long-gone but not forgotten, her only kin had left too soon, and sad memories

brought tears trickling down her cheeks. "Mamira," she cried, her lonely years

a gaping wound. Overcome with grief and misery, she could do naught but freeze,

heart aching beyond what she could bear. She keened, willing to give anything—

do anything—to see her mother again, feel her tight hug, and hear the familiar

"Beloved Zizi, I'm truly blessed that you're my child." Her mother used to sing

those words to her, saying them repeatedly, too. The memory was so very real,

she moaned, but still savored it, closing her eyes. Warmth enveloped her and

something caressed her cheek, like her parent used to do. She could almost feel

Mamira's presence and opened her eyes, a whimper escaping from her lips when

she saw the translucent figure standing there. "I've missed you so much," she

sobbed, rushing to hug her. But the girl's arms passed through the woman then.

"Don't fret, sweet child." The words were soft but quite clear. "It's to be expected,

since I died. But I'm here with you now, and with your help, maybe I can remain."

"You didn't just die," Aziza replied. "You were *killed*. The village council directed

people to stone you and called you a witch, but you'd done no wrong. They're doing

the same thing to Marda, and she has no power at all." But Mamira's words penetrated,

74

and the girl went quiet, frowning. *"Remain?"* Her mother sighed. "I've been ruing

not revealing myself, but I had to wait until you were ready." Looking up, she pointed.

"That is a blood moon. Under it, those who have magic are at their strongest, and your

power has been surfacing, hasn't it?" She didn't wait for a reply. "You were anointed

as a baby. Destined for greatness. I waited forever for you, our sisterhood, too." Only

then did Aziza realize many more ghosts—witches—had appeared, watching. Listening.

Mamira began chanting unknown words. The rest joined in, and Aziza felt heat gradually

suffusing her. Tingling spread throughout her body, increased, and she wondered if liquid

fire coursed through her veins. Sparks flew from her eyes. Flames danced on her skin, and

things she'd never known filled her mind, but they felt as normal to her as breathing did.

Words came to her, and she spoke them in unison with the other women. "Mighty Goddess,

hear our plea. We have honored thee. Served thee. And we would willingly do so forever.

But our enemies robbed us of our lives. Robbed us from thy service. We humbly confess

we seek vengeance and cannot succeed without thy aid. We

seek the predicted restoration,

and beg thee to please give strength and abundance to us now, especially to young Aziza."

Moonlight pierced the canopy overhead, landing on the girl, who fell to her knees, adoration

for her mother uppermost in her mind. Having Mamira back would be a dream come true,

and she pleaded with the Goddess, offering her life freely or to serve for the rest of it—if only…

Thunder sounded in the distance, the ground shaking under Aziza's feet. Gusts of wind blew,

and jagged bolts of lightning split the sky. Suddenly, without any warning, the moon turned

a blinding white, and rays shot down, illuminating the girl. Her eyes mirrored the glow, and

she stood frozen as power poured into her. The light finally vanished, but her body burned,

the flesh not being consumed. Flames danced in her eyes and on her skin. She pointed at her

mother, energy coursing from her to the woman, then brought the others back to life also.

Once finished, her fire vanished, but compared to a normal person, her eyes shone brighter.

In town, some villagers discussed the mysterious lights, others the individual they were

stoning. They gaped, seeing women approaching, Aziza in

the lead, her mother beside her.

People grabbed rocks, knives, spears—any weapon. *"Kill them!"* town leaders screamed.

But their savage glee turned into horror when they saw how all the witches' eyes gleamed.

Smiling, the women shot fire from their fingertips. People went up in flames, shrieks and

wails rising everywhere. "You'll never hurt us again," Aziza yelled. "And this is *our* land!"

 **The Siamese**

A WHITE SIAMESE cat sauntered along the beach. Stopping, it looked at the waves rolling in from the Pacific, the churning surf, and the people going to and from the water.

Seagulls standing near the shoreline glanced at the white animal before flying away.

"What did I tell you?" The blonde man pointed toward the feline. "Everyone in California loves the ocean and beach. Even cats do."

His redheaded friend shrugged. "I figured fewer people would be out, since it's Halloween."

"Nope. They come all the time." Propping his surfboard against a nearby concession stand, the blonde said, "Give me a piece of your hot dog."

"Hey, I only have one bite left." His pal frowned. "I got this for myself, not some stray cat."

"Don't be selfish. You can get more later. Heck, you can get ten hot dogs if you want. The cat needs food more than you do. Look how skinny he is."

"Oh, all right." Making a face, the redhead stooped and held out his offering. "If you're hungry, come get it." The animal stared at him but made no move in his direction. "Come here, kitty, kitty, kitty. I've got something for you."

The Siamese continued to study him but didn't budge.

"Gimme that." The blonde took the portion of food, slowly approaching the white animal. "Don't be afraid, dude. I won't hurt you." Shoving back locks of his hair which had fallen across his forehead, he knelt beside the feline. "You hungry?" After the cat gently took the food from the proffered hand, devouring it in a flash, the man petted the furry head, then stood. "Well, we gotta go, but you take care, little buddy. If you're still here later, I'll buy you your own hot dog."

The animal watched them enter the water, then hissed as it nimbly avoided being smacked by a kayak two women drug across the sand. Other people dressed up as ghouls and zombies passed by, carrying jet skis. Ignoring them, the cat walked away. It continued until it reached a deserted area of beach and moved toward a house on the right which had figures in the front yard.

As the feline padded across the lawn, a witch standing there cackled. The Frankenstein beside it growled ominously. The cat ignored both Halloween decorations, going around them and a coffin, which began to open.

Short-fuse, the Chihuahua who lived here, napped in a chair on the porch. One of his ears twitched, then the other. Raising his head, he spied the newcomer, jumped out of the chair, and ran across the porch and down the steps, letting out piercing yaps all the way.

The Siamese stopped to watch the approaching dog.

When Short-fuse was close enough, he lunged at the cat. The feline deftly avoided his attack, extended its claws, and raked them across the canine's nose. Short-fuse squealed. Rubbing his injured nose on the ground, he growled, and ran at the intruder. Evading the dog, the Siamese scratched him a second time. The Chihuahua yelped but still tried once more—unsuccessfully.

Without any warning, the cat dashed away toward a stand of sequoias and redwoods nearby. It leapt onto a trunk and climbed up high. Short-fuse ran frantically back and forth at the base of the tree, yapping even louder. The Siamese clung to the trunk, claws embedded firmly, and stared down at the noisemaker.

Breaking into one frenzied burst of barking after another, the dog vibrated all over, as though an electrical current flowed through him. He practically bounced up and down.

Turning its head first one direction, then the other, the white cat scanned its surroundings. No one was around— no person, at least—although sandpipers ran this way and that. Focusing on the excited animal emitting staccato yips below, the feline opened its mouth, and a green tongue— several feet long—shot out toward the ground.

The dog didn't notice at first. However, seeing the long appendage split at the end, his eyes widened, and he stopped moving.

Using its forked tongue to snatch up Short-fuse, the Siamese pulled him back toward its mouth. The dog barely

81

had time to whine before the cat's mouth expanded to gulp him down.

Off to the right, the front door to the house opened. A woman stepped outside, looked around, and called out, "Short-fuse! Here, boy. Come here, puppy, puppy!" He didn't appear, so she yelled, "Short-fuse! Where are you?" She spoke over her shoulder, "Bud, I heard Short-fuse barking his head off at something, but now he's gone. Do you think he ran off again?" When she received no reply, she frowned. "*Bud*, did you hear me?"

"Yeah," a man responded. "I'm sure he's fine."

"You're probably right but remember how mad the neighbors got when he went after their guinea pig. You don't think they'd..."

"Stop fretting. That stupid yapper is always running after something. Birds, seals, crabs. He'll return like he always does. Come back and watch this movie with me."

"All right. I'm coming."

The Siamese with a tummy full of now-silent Chihuahua released its claw-hold on the tree trunk, dropping to the earth. Stretching languidly, it gave a deep burp.

Glancing at the house, the cat noted a piece of lopsided siding moving beneath the porch. A tabby poked her head out, caught sight of the other animal, and uttered a mewl.

Padding that direction, the Siamese sat a few feet from the porch, extended one leg into the air, and groomed itself with a normal-looking tongue. The tabby made an inquisitive, questioning sound. Licking one toe after another, the white cat replied with a confident meow. The tabby took a hesitant step forward, stopping to scent the air in the stranger's direction.

Opening its mouth, the Siamese spoke in a friendly human voice. "Come here, kitty, kitty, kitty."

The tabby cocked her head to the side, and then moved closer.

 The Devil's Hand

ANGELINE IMAGINED HOW Shane would react tomorrow—how dismayed he'd be—and grinned. No way he'd be able to break his word, though, since their entire English class had heard him. Remembering what happened, she smirked.

He'd uttered a high-pitched squeal when a spider scurried across his desk, and everyone had died laughing. Spiders didn't bother Angeline, so she'd killed it and disposed of the body. Their classmates had teased him, calling him a "wuss" and "little girl," but praised her, saying she was fearless. No doubt that's why he'd dared her to spend the night in The Devil's Hand. "Why should she?" someone had asked, her friends demanding, "What's in it for her?" Shane had promised she could use his Dodge Charger for a week if she succeeded. Royal blue with flames on the sides, the sportscar was fairly new with spinning wheels and a phenomenal sound system. It was a hundred times nicer than the old truck her parents let her drive, and she couldn't wait to claim the keys.

Since seventeen-year-old Angeline loved camping, she wasn't worried about staying overnight in the Hand, which lay on a tree-covered hill several miles outside of town. Five tall but narrow boulders protruded from the earth there in a circular pattern, each leaning inward slightly and closely resembling fingers protruding from the ground. Some people said the spot was haunted, others that it was cursed. According to legend, Druids had considered it a sacred site, and a witches' coven had held ceremonies there. Several individuals claimed to have seen ghosts. A few spoke of people who'd gone missing through the years. One man swore he'd followed Bigfoot into the area before the creature vanished.

Angeline chalked everything up as hype designed to bolster the town's notoriety and attract tourists. It made sense, since she knew magical things were just a bunch of hooey.

After pitching her tent, she gathered wood for a fire and soon had it blazing. Not that she needed the warmth. She just liked the smell of burning wood. She wolfed down the now-cool burger and tater tots she'd brought with her, chasing down bites with her rather runny chocolate shake.

She listened to the night sounds—crickets, frogs, owls, a wail that might've been a bobcat, and coyotes howling in the distance—but didn't hear anything unusual. The moon was obscured by clouds, but the stars overhead formed a canopy, seeming much clearer and brighter than from home. It was so nice outside, she decided not to use her tent at all, and moved her sleeping bag over by the fire.

Angeline drifted off to sleep thinking of all the pictures

she'd take of herself with Shane's car, and the places she'd drive.

In her dreams, she won the lottery, bought her own Charger—a bright red one—and everyone oohed and ahhed over it. She heard their murmurs and opened her eyes. More asleep than awake, she smelled something sweet and cloying, and her head swam, her thoughts fuzzy. The nearby stone fingers seemed to be moving, and she snickered at the ludicrous thought. Unable to keep her eyelids from sagging, she fell asleep again.

Angeline heard chanting and yawned, secure in the knowledge she was still dreaming. Strangely, her body felt damp all over as if she'd just gotten out of the shower or been sweating for hours. Sweat trickled down her forehead and she wiped it away. Forcing her eyes open, she saw people moving around several feet away. She blinked, straining to see their faces, but they were hidden in the shadows.

Her feet were uncomfortably warm, and she flexed them, grimacing. But she gasped when she looked down, discovering she was in a large pot filled with water. A fire blazed underneath it.

"Get me out of here!" she shouted.

Figures approached, and she flinched, seeing their misshapen heads and green skin. Tusks protruded from their mouths, and their arms were abnormally long. They must've been a few feet taller than people and made her think of fairy tales she'd read as a kid. Were they trolls? Monsters?

One dropped wild onions into the pot, and she realized potatoes, carrots, and other vegetables already floated there. Another of the beings studied her, licking its lips.

"Help!" Angeline yelled as loudly as she could. "Someone, help me! *Please!"*

A monster snarled, baring its teeth, and grabbed a branch off the ground, walloping her with it.

Dazed, her ears rang, and her head pounded. The creature used the branch to shove her head underwater, and everything went black.

 **True Beauty**

EIGHTEEN-YEAR-OLD Tricia carefully plucked her eyebrows, applied eye shadow, eyeliner, and mascara, lip liner and lipstick, and the slightest hint of blush on her cheeks. Picking up one of the bottles of expensive perfume lining the makeup table in front of her, she raised it to her nose, sniffed it, then smelled a few others. She chose the most expensive—a gift from an ex-boyfriend she'd dumped after meeting a wealthier man—and dabbed some on her neck and wrists.

Next came a pair of jewel-studded earrings and the matching necklace, presents from her new admirer—a forty-two-year-old, married man. Then she studied her rings. He'd let her choose from among the costliest at the jewelry stores. "Only the best for me," she gloated aloud. After all, she deserved everything she already had and much, much more. Last week, he'd paid a year's rent in advance on an apartment just for her, and she planned to cajole a sportscar out of him next.

They'd had such a nice time at the restaurant last night, except for one minor detail. Bonnie, a loser from Tricia's high school, worked there. Tricia's lips stretched into a sneer as she thought of all the enjoyment she and her friends had gotten from messing with the other girl. They'd treated her like the dog she was, and it had always been fun.

Tricia shuddered at the thought of putting her own hands—with their perfect, soft skin—into something as awful as dishwater. "Ick," she said aloud, grimacing in horror. And she wouldn't dream of working, especially not when others could give her what she wanted.

Running a comb through her blonde hair, she admired its long, silky smoothness. "I'm glad I'm beautiful," she gloated. "Bonnie's so ugly. And she's such a fat cow." She couldn't have cared less about the fact that the other girl's father had died the previous year, and Bonnie had gone to work to help support her family.

***

Across town, Bonnie huddled in her bed after reading the latest Facebook messages. Tears streaked the seventeen-year-old's face, and sobs shook her body. If anything, the latest posts were more hateful than the others she'd received over the past few months.

Sniffling, she picked up her journal and wrote: "*I saw Tricia talking to my manager at work last night. She told him she saw me taking the servers' tips from their tables. I'd never do* that, but the manager fired me anyway. Now I have to find another job. Today was awful, too. Someone shoved me from behind in P.E. right as I was about to jump a hurdle, and I fell. Tricia and the other mean girls took pictures of me on the ground and posted them on Facebook. They said I'm a short, fat, clumsy troll, and they're right. My shirt had gone up over my belly and it looked huge. My mouth was hanging open like a dying fish. Everyone's going to laugh at me even more now. I just can't do anything right. I don't know why I joined the hurdle team or thought I could succeed at anything. I've been trying to feel better about myself, but I really am ugly, fat, and clumsy. Tricia said I'm nothing but a worthless loser and should do everyone a favor and kill myself. Maybe she's right. What's the point of being alive anymore? I should just get it over with."

She found a mostly full bottle of Mom's anti-depressant in the medicine cabinet. As she swallowed pill after pill, she thought of her mother, who hadn't gotten home yet, and her father, who was gone forever. They were loving and kind people who always told her she was lovely and smart and could succeed at whatever she wanted. But they were her parents. They had to say that.

Bonnie wrote a short note and started to feel tired. She managed one final word, "Goodbye," before her eyes grew too heavy. She lay down on her bed and stopped trying to stay awake.

***

Tricia donned a new party dress and admired herself in the mirror, blowing her reflection a kiss. She shrieked when someone materialized behind her with no warning.

Whirling, she stared wide-eyed at the beautiful, black-haired woman.

***

"Vain, heartless creature," Ria hissed, not waiting for the girl to speak.

"How'd you get in my room?" Tricia demanded. "Who are you?"

"I've gone by many things, including Ria, but Justice or Vengeance is the most fitting." Glancing at a roll of paper towels nearby, Ria gave a slight nod. A few sheets tore apart and shot across the room into Tricia's open mouth, preventing a reply.

Ria pointed toward Tricia's makeup table. The cap on her mascara unscrewed itself, and the wand lifted into the air to poke the girl's cheek. She winced and tried to get away but found herself unable to move her legs and feet. The wand hit again—harder this time—puncturing Tricia's skin. She whimpered as blood trickled from the injury. A container of eye shadow flew through the air, and one corner struck her shoulder, leaving a deep scratch. The soft lipstick Tricia had used only moments ago whipped toward her, hardening, and jabbed her in the chin with its now-sharp edge.

Under the barrage of even more makeup, Tricia struggled to get free of Ria's power, but couldn't. Arms flailing wildly, she tried to knock away the attacking cosmetics, her cries and yells muffled by the paper towels. But her beauty produces stabbed her over and over, leaving

92

her with dozens of wounds.

"Enough going easy on you," Ria snarled, eyes narrowed. She extended one slender hand, which turned into a tiger's paw, tipped with curved, vicious claws. Then she lashed out to rip a strip of flesh from Tricia's face. The girl screamed in pain, trembling all over. Ria slashed again and again, then slowly drew the tip of one claw along her captive's hairline. When she was finished, she held up a dripping scalp.

Tricia wailed through the tissue in her mouth, then fell to her knees. Ignoring the sounds, Ria studied the mangled wreckage of what had formerly been a stunning visage. "Not so high and mighty now, are you?"

Locating the girl's phone, Ria used it to take pictures and posted them to Facebook. Then she vanished.

She reappeared at the comatose Bonnie's side and snapped her fingers. The teenager's eyes popped open, and she vomited. Ria found a washcloth in the bathroom, wet it with warm water, and gently washed Bonnie's pale face.

Staring into the girl's wide eyes, Ria caught her spark of hope and belief and held it. "You have true beauty. Never let anyone tell you differently. And you will never, ever, try to harm yourself again."

 **Surviving**

"FINALLY!" **VERA RUSHED** toward her twelve-year-old daughter, Marianne, hugging her fiercely before grabbing her husband, Cole. "What happened? Y'all were supposed to return yesterday morning." She talked fast, almost babbling. "I couldn't eat or relax the whole time you were gone. Horrible scenarios kept running through my..."

Cole interrupted. "We're safe, Sweetheart, just like I said we'd be."

She studied him, expression still troubled. "Thank God."

"We got bark, roots, and some wild onions I'll plant in the garden. Hopefully, they'll thrive."

"What about meat? Did you catch a rabbit or squirrel?"

"No, but we will another day. Right now, I'm *starving.*" Turning down the corners of his mouth, Cole rubbed his belly, uttering an exaggerated moan. "My stomach feels like it's eating itself from the inside out."

"Mine, too." Marianne grinned.

"Go clean up, young lady. You're wearing so much dirt, it looks like you rolled on the ground." Winking, her father playfully tapped her nose, and she left giggling. But his smile and jovial attitude vanished once as she was out of sight.

"It's bad, isn't it?" Vera asked.

"Yeah. The stores were stripped bare months ago, but the other stuff was gone, too."

"The things you couldn't carry last time and hid?"

Cole nodded. "And the trees are gone."

"*All* of them?"

"People probably have been burning wood for warmth, since it's been so cold. They even dug up the stumps and roots. And we didn't see any animals. Not a bird flying. Not a possum or stray dog. We searched for plants, but zilch, just like when you tried before. We had to go further out. That's why we took longer."

"While y'all were gone, I did some digging, but didn't find any grubs, worms, anything. The ground was hard—I guess from the drought and winter temperatures. Maybe it's time to move."

"We were lucky, finding this underground storm shelter. Luckier it's well-hidden. And if not for the sleeping bags and Sterno, we would've needed another heat source."

"Surely we can find another place."

"I don't know. From what I've heard, supplies are sparse to nonexistent everywhere. So are safe places. Just looking around is dangerous because of…"

"The rovers."

"Yeah. Several miles away, I saw large warehouses, but they're bound to be occupied."

"You think the rovers are living there?"

"Most likely."

"How are the others?"

"Martin and Shelley left. No one knows when or where they went. Sean, Mary, and their son are okay, but George and Carrie are gone."

"We could stay in that basement where they'd been."

"No. When I said gone, I meant *dead.*" Vera gasped. "Someone broke in and killed them."

"Is Jayson all right?"

"Shhh. Marianne's coming."

"I decided what to fix," their daughter announced. It was her turn to do the meal. She boiled bark and mint leaves in water to make tea, divided it into three portions, and opened a can of pork and beans for them to share.

Soon after, they were grabbing their stomachs, vomiting, and having diarrhea.

"We knew that might happen," Cole whispered after Marianne dozed off, still groaning in her sleep.

"I know." Vera's voice shook. "But not from canned food. Whoever contaminated those batches of cans did it months before everything fell apart. I thought stores took the bad stuff off their shelves."

"I'm sure they did, but more things could've been contaminated with nobody realizing it."

"Or maybe the pork and beans didn't make us sick. It could've been the bark or mint, right? Since radiation spreads?"

"Anything's possible. But I'm almost certain it was the beans. Not from radiation, though. I checked the can. It was well past the expiration date and discolored at the bottom."

Frowning, Vera went to examine their supplies. "We only have eight gallons of water, nine cans of vegetables, and eleven of fruit, but if any or all of them are bad..."

"Everything will be okay. I'm leaving tomorrow. Just me. I'll be gone two days. Maybe three. But we'll be okay, Vera. I promise."

"Where are you going?" She narrowed her eyes at him, but he glanced away. "Cole, look at me. *Where?*" She bit her lip, voice quavering. "You plan to go to The Field, don't you?"

"I have no choice."

"Yes, you do. We agreed, remember? It's dangerous."

"We need food."

"That isn't food."

"Vera."

"The other cans are probably fine."

"Even if they are, they won't feed us for long. Then what?"

"What if the rovers see you?"

"I'll be careful, and I'll take the gun with me."

"That isn't good enough, Cole. They'd *kill* you. In their eyes, you'd be nothing but fresh meat."

"I doubt they'd be interested in me, since bodies are added to The Field daily. And I'm sure to find one in good shape."

"Maybe they're contaminated."

"They aren't."

"You don't know that. And lying to reassure me just makes me worry more."

"Okay. They *could* be contaminated, but everyone must be by now."

"Your eyes—I can tell you're still hiding something from me."

His shoulders drooped. "I found out last week, and I didn't tell you because... Sit down, Honey." After she did, he admitted, "It's Jayson."

"The rovers injured him?"

Shaking his head, Cole slid an arm around her waist, his voice going flat. "He killed himself."

"*No!*" Clapping her hands over her mouth, she stifled a scream. "He wouldn't—couldn't. He believes in doing what's right, and knows suicide's wrong."

But she read the truth on his face, and tears poured down her cheeks. "He's—he *was*—*my* last relative except for you and Marianne. Mom and Dad—dead. My grandparents, other brothers, sister—dead. How could he do this to me?" She began sobbing hysterically.

"I'm so sorry, Honey." Cole held her tightly, muffling her cries. "I know it's devastating, but Jayson didn't do it to hurt you. He was between a rock and a hard place, and I'm sure the only thing on his mind was his wife and kids

99

starving. Remember how weak they'd gotten? With him dead, they'd have meat."

"Meat?" Yanking away, Vera punched his chest. "He's my big brother, not *meat!*"

He tried to hold her again, but she resisted. Within seconds, though, she buried her face in his shoulder.

The next day

"Read it before you go, Daddy," Marianne urged. "Please."

"You've heard it dozens of times." Vera frowned. "How about a story instead?" She rummaged through a pile of books, scanning the spines. "Tolkien? Keene? We've got Texas history, gardening, romances, fantasies."

"No. I want to hear what Daddy wrote. I know it's unhappy, but it's our lives, Mama. My life."

Cole squeezed Vera's shoulder, went for his journal, and began reading.

"March 17, 2026. Vera and I worried when COVID-19 kept spreading in 2020. But we thought it'd eventually go away, with things returning to normal. The majority of Americans believed that, but it didn't happen. During the first two years alone, the virus mutated more than once, each mutation resulting in more cases. More deaths. The pattern held true throughout the next three years, and officials claimed it had mutated fourteen times. We knew people who tested positive with nasty symptoms while others were asymptomatic, seeming healthy as could be. Many got through quarantine successfully, then caught COVID again. Vera and I did, and both our kids.

We paid close attention to the number of cases in Texas,

our state. Despite another lockdown, they rose, skyrocketing further out of control. Texas was reeling. The entire United States was, but it wasn't the only nation. The world as a whole was brought to its knees, ninety-seven percent of inhabitants experiencing the loss of someone close, according to estimates. People's ability to work and earn money had already been impacted, but worse yet, death continued stealing away loved ones left and right."

"Harry," Marianne murmured.

"Yes," Vera whispered. "Your brother would've been eight..." She walked into their small, makeshift kitchen.

Cole cleared his throat and continued reading. "Everyone blamed the government for not doing more. But I doubt they knew what to do. Millions of dollars had already been poured into research and vaccines. People said someone had to be responsible, that the virus was too pervasive and resistant to be naturally-occurring. Vera and I had our theories, too.

Experts originally claimed eighty-five percent of the infected recovered, but by the second year, a solid thirty-two percent of the populace were dying. The percentage rose from there. Reporters said it hit forty-seven percent eventually, then stopped saying. By the time scientists overseas announced their "miracle cure," everyone fell over themselves offering up their arms for shots. We tried to get them, but supplies had run out. That turned out to be good, though. The so-called medicine had been designed to create a short-term energy boost and euphoria while insidiously damaging bodies from the inside out. But no one knew that until it was too late.

The ensuing wave of deaths spread from town to town,

101

state to state, and around the globe, and the majority of those who were left had permanent impairments. Diseases to virus-induced aches and pains, on through new but here-to stay brain fog."

"And then the attack happened," Marianne said, glancing at her mother, who'd returned and nodded slowly.

"Unknown enemies struck the United States," Cole read. "They hacked our nation's computers, took over the Treasury, stock market, and gained access to nuclear codes. Our government took a series of actions to catch the culprits and restore order, but the value of our dollar took a hit. Our economy crashed, taking with it many companies which produced food, gas, and water. Supplies became harder and harder to find. Protests and riots rocked the same cities as before, but spread to others which were formerly peaceful. The President announced they'd regained control of everything, and promised to help companies and families get to their feet, but everything was in shambles. And that wasn't even the worst of it."

"Nuclear bombs hit American soil for the first time." Vera sat by Cole, putting her arm around his shoulders.

He sighed and kissed her cheek. "They were our own bombs. Hackers—terrorists—had control after all, and targeted major cities. Hundreds of thousands died immediately, others suffering the effects of radiation. Dallas was one of the first places hit. We're two hours away but knew the radiation would spread. Martial law was instated to keep things from worsening, but they did anyway. Food shortages led to break-ins, attacks, thefts. Our house was burned, but we'd already left. Any semblance of law and order gave way. Citizens turned on one another and the rest, as they say, is history."

"Gami and Gramps died." Marianne hiccupped, tears rolling down her cheeks. "I miss them."

Dad cleared his throat again. A tear trickled down his face and Vera wiped it away. "They were in Houston, another place hit first. I miss them, too." He began to read again, "We..."

"No." Vera shook her head. "That's enough. I can't... It's just—too much."

Five days later

"I'm so happy to see you." Vera threw her arms around Cole, Marianne following suit.

Cole hugged them tightly, set down his backpack, and pointed at it. "Meat," he announced succinctly. "Marianne, would you dig up two or three potatoes from the garden? A turnip and onion, too. I'm going to fix stew." Once she hurried away, he staggered, leaning heavily on his wife.

She yanked his jacket open and blanched. "You're injured." She examined the wound. "A bullet hole."

He gritted his teeth. "It went straight through without hitting bone or anything vital. Marianne doesn't need to know. Not yet anyway. She'll have enough to deal with soon."

"What do you mean?" After he explained, she vomited, then snapped, *"No! Never!"*

"Listen to me." Cole's voice rasped. "No new bodies were in The Field, and the ones there were stripped bare. Nothing left but bones. Rovers came out of nowhere and I barely got away. If I hadn't had my gun... Luckily, they weren't good shots. I killed one and cut chunks of flesh off

103

of him, but I didn't have time to get more. What I brought will only last so long, and you know we've already been getting weaker."

Six days later

Cole swayed on his feet, but held Marianne who bawled like a baby.

"I thought Mama loved me," she sobbed. "How could she leave me?"

"She left us both, Honey." Her father's voice cracked. "She loves—loved—us deeply, and that's why she did this. I probably shouldn't tell you, but I'd planned to kill myself so y'all would have food." His daughter gasped and looked horrified. "I told your mother she'd have to remove my flesh and smoke it quickly, so it wouldn't go bad. So it'd last."

Marianne's face crumpled. "People aren't food. *They're —people.*"

"I know, but we have nothing to eat except one piece of bark, two potatoes, and an onion plant. Your mother left a note saying I was better equipped to keep you safe. She knew I'd stay alive if she were gone. She knew I'd never, ever leave you alone."

"So she killed herself instead."

Cole began sobbing, too, body shaking as he held Marianne close. "Yes."

 Gotcha

"WHAT YOU'RE DOING is wrong," Charlie said, voice shaking. "Don't you understand that? Please listen…"

"Shut up, old man," Dean retorted. When his grandfather winced and tightened his lips, the eighteen-year-old sneered, raising both of his middle fingers before storming out of the house.

Charlie sighed. His daughter Mary and her husband Ron had been good people—the definition of salt-of-the-earth, in his opinion—and good role models to Dean, but their son had been trouble from an early age. He'd disobeyed more than he'd listened, bullied other kids for no reason, and they'd caught him torturing animals. In the last few years, he'd escalated into committing robbery and assault, often acting violently toward his own parents, too. They'd taken him to counselors and psychiatrists, experts who dealt with behavioral issues, and even sought out ministers, but nothing they'd tried had changed his behavior.

Both of Dean's parents had died in a house fire shortly after he turned seventeen. The police had learned of their plans to put him in long-term residential treatment— something about which he'd been angry—and suspected the boy of arson and murder but hadn't found enough proof. At sixty-two, Charlie had received custody of the teenager, but hadn't really believed he was capable of what he was accused of. Law enforcement's description of Dean as a "sociopath" had shaken him, but he'd learned it wasn't an exaggeration. His grandson hadn't been with him all that long when people in his neighborhood began complaining about him bullying their children and luring their pets to him, only to shoot them with his BB-gun, kick them, or do other equally mean things. A few animals had vanished altogether. Charlie had his suspicions about that, and constantly worried what the kid would do next.

***

Josh hid behind the bushes and snickered. His best friends, Ned and Will, wouldn't think to look for him in this greenhouse, even though Old Man Charlie Wilson had caught the eleven-year-olds playing Hide and Seek here two days ago. They always searched for new hiding spots, and this one had been perfect, but Charlie had fussed as if their being there was the end of the world. He'd gone on and on about his Venus Fly Traps, and how easily the boys could damage them, even if they didn't intend to. Then he'd threatened to call their parents if they came back. Josh knew his friends were wimps and wouldn't take a chance on getting in trouble.

"We give up!" Ned and Will yelled from somewhere outside.

Coming out of hiding, Josh grinned at the thought of rubbing their noses in his victory. But he stiffened when someone stepped in front of him.

"Whatcha doing, loser?" Dean sneered before snatching Josh's hat off his head.

"Give it back!" Josh demanded. His dad had given him that hat before he died in a wreck the prior year. "That's mine."

"What'd you say?" Dean punched him in the gut and left, wearing Josh's hat on his own head.

Four days later

"I'm glad you asked permission this time, Ned," Charlie said. "Venus Fly Traps are truly fascinating. Come with me. I'll tell you a little bit about them."

The boys followed him into the greenhouse. Ned and Will edged closer to the plants, hanging on the old man's every word, but Josh hung back, his shoulders sagging. In his dream last night, Dad came home and hugged him the way he always used to. Josh had been so relieved and excited, but that excitement had died when he woke up and realized the truth. Touching his dad's cap used to help him feel close to his father and give him comfort, but he couldn't do that anymore.

"Those things eat people, right?" Will asked.

Charlie laughed. "No. Where'd you get that idea?"

"Because they're cardy... carny..." Ned stuttered.

"Carnivorous?" Charlie asked.

"Yeah. That's the word."

"They *are* carnivorous and enjoy an occasional fly or insect, but they're way too small to eat people. Look at their size compared to ours... It's important you steer clear of this greenhouse if I'm not here. I make money raising these plants, and I'll be really upset to see any of them hurt. Y'hear me, boys?"

***

Three weeks later, Charlie walked into the greenhouse to prepare an order of Venus Fly Traps and froze, gasping. The leaves on several had been torn. Others had fallen off. Rocks lay scattered on the ground, as if someone had thrown them at his plants. "Poor things," he murmured, crooning to them as he examined them tenderly, and he used great care in applying medicinal salve to the leaves. Living things responded to kindness, he believed, and his plants did better when he spoke to them.

Several minutes later, he watched the neighborhood boys playing nearby, chattering, and laughing as they threw a baseball back and forth. Charlie knew in his heart they'd done nothing wrong. But he could guess who had.

When he came back an hour later, he caught Dean throwing rocks at his plants again.

"Stop that!" Charlie snapped, getting between them and the delinquent. "These are living things, Dean, and they're paying the bills. I didn't raise them for you to destroy."

"Drop dead." Dean pelted his grandfather with rocks

108

now.

"Will you stop? There's a right and a wrong and..." Another stone hit the side of Charlie's head, and he swayed on his feet. He leaned on the wall, and heard his grandson laughing as he walked away.

***

Two weeks later

"I bet Josh is in the greenhouse again," Ned said. "That's where he hid last time, remember?"

"Charlie said to keep out," Will argued. "And I don't want Dad fussing at me. Mom either."

"He won't know. None of them will."

They didn't find Josh inside but were captivated when they looked around and saw all the good spots they could hide. Young trees and bushes were clustered here and there. A tractor sat off to the left, and there were piles of pallets, fertilizer, and other things. It didn't take them long to start playing. They took turns hiding, chased each other around, periodically chucked clods of dirt at one another, but carefully avoided the Venus Fly Trap beds on the right.

Will had just tackled Ned when the door creaked open. They were quick to hide, not wanting Charlie to catch them and get upset.

"Come out, jerk wads." It was Dean, not Charlie.

They glanced at each other, silently agreeing to stay hidden.

"I know you're in here," the bully said. "I saw you enter.

109

You better show yourselves. If you don't, you're gonna be sorry." Minutes passed but they didn't. As he began searching for them, Ned and Bill steadily repositioned themselves, staying as far away from him as possible. When they were finally near the door, they crawled toward it, eased it open, and fled.

"I got you now," Dean yelled as the door creaked shut. "You just wait till I get my hands on you." He raced toward the exit, but still didn't find them. He didn't see them outside when he glanced around and went back inside the greenhouse.

As he stalked around, he heard a faint sound to his right, and charged that direction. He walked between two Venus Fly Trap beds, didn't see anyone, and shrugged. Then a faint snapping sound reached his ears. It came from behind him. "You're breaking twigs?" he demanded. "You dipshits are gonna regret messing with me."

A sound like exhaled air came from his left. "Here I come!" he crowed and dashed toward it.

Behind him, a large Venus Fly Trap swayed without making any noise. A pair of eyes opened up in its blossom, and more sets appeared in the other plants. Loud rustling could be heard, coming from everywhere.

"Now you're making me mad," Dean snarled. Glancing at the Venus Fly Traps—the eyes had disappeared—he grimaced. "Ugly things. Next time, I'll finish you off." He turned his back on them.

Pulling its roots out of the ground, the largest Venus Fly Trap silently moved toward the bully, and its bulb expanded to many times its original size. The plant darted forward, snatched Dean off his feet, and dropped him amid the other plants. The boy yelled and tried to get up, but they closed in rapidly, biting him and tearing huge chunks of flesh from his body. His terrified screams stopped short once his head was ripped from his shoulders.

***

The greenhouse door opened, and Josh peeked in. "Ned? Will? Do you give up?" They didn't answer and he started to shut the door.

Something flew up out of the plants and hit the ground with a soft thud.

Josh walked toward the sound. "Guys, is that you?" He cocked his head when he noticed something lying on the soil and went for a closer look. Then he realized it was his dad's hat.

"Hey!" he exclaimed. Bending to grab it, he placed it on his head with a grin.

The End.

You may read more about the author and her other works on the following pages.

<u>Gabriella Balcom</u>

Gabriella Balcom lives in Texas with her family, works full-time in the mental health field, and has loved reading and writing her entire life. She writes fantasy, horror, sci-fi, romance, literary fiction, children's stories, and more, and loves great stories, forests, mountains, and back roads. She has a weakness for lasagna, garlic bread, tacos, cheese, and chocolate, but not necessarily in that order, and adores Chinese, Italian, and Mexican food. Gabriella has had 350 works accepted for publication, and won the right to have a novel published by Clarendon House Publications when one of her short stories was voted best in the anthology in which it appeared. Her book, On the Wings of Ideas, came out afterward. She was nominated for the Washington Science Fiction Association's Small Press Award, and won second place in The JayZoMon Dark Myth Company's 2020 Open Contract Challenge (a competition in which around one hundred authors competed for cash prizes and publishing contracts). Gabriella's novelette, Worth Waiting For, was then released. She self-published a novelette, Free's Tale: No Home at Christmas-time, and Black Hare Press published her sci-fi novella, The Return, in 2021. Five other novellas pend publication. You are invited to visit her Facebook author page: https://m.facebook.com/GabriellaBalcom.lonestarauthor.

Information about Gabriella's other books is on the following pages.

Other Books by Gabriella Balcom

On the Wings of Ideas

Some authors have a range so wide and a scope so varied that it's difficult to 'pin them down' in a few words. Best-selling author Gabriella Balcom can write science fiction, fantasy, children's literature, literary fiction, poetry, horror, humor, romance, and more—and you'll find all of the above in this eclectic collection of tales…

She won the publishing contract for this anthology after one of her stories was voted best in the novel in which it first appeared. Her book includes the following and more:

*** Jakob has survived everything life's thrown at him: being forced to grow up too fast, poverty, and military service. But can he survive his beloved mother's death-bed request?

*** Ralph deteriorates more by the day, and Gertrude is devastated. She'd do anything to save him, even sneak into a top-secret facility.

*** Serial killers fascinate young Bobby, and he's developed some rather unusual hobbies of his own. No one knows. No one would ever guess.

Gabriella Balcom

*** Edwina and her classmates are storming Area 51, but she feels like vomiting. They see this as an adventure to boast about, but for her, it's a matter of life and death.

*** Sandy struggles with low self-esteem, and has good reason to resent a specific person. But she's shocked when a supernatural being gives her a chance for some well-deserved payback.

*** Mei longs for a baby more than life itself, and appeals to a goddess for help.

*** Dahlya wants to help an injured cat, but her widowed father knows he can't afford to feed it. He can barely keep himself and his daughter fed and housed.

*** Maggie stresses about Joe constantly. If anything happens to her, who would take care of him?

*** Sluuge has been trapped behind the Boundary for eons. However, everything is going to change soon, because the magical barrier is about to come down.

*** Ruth's attempt to save a badly damaged rose plant has consequences, and she's unexpectedly transported to a marvelous, magical world.

*** Becky the Blabbermouth delights in trouble-making, doing so every chance she gets. However, she's about to learn karma is quite real.

*** Sylana hides in terror when He appears. Will her invisibility and protection spells work? Is a war about to begin? Sometimes nothing is what it seems.

*** Jenny tries and tries, but can't write a good story about fairies, and travels to Ireland for inspiration. If only magical creatures were real…

*** Kevin's discovery shocks him. Could that be—a

monster?

The paperback version is available here:

https://www.amazon.com/gp/aw/d/B0898Z8FJN/ref=tmm_p
ap_title_0?ie=UTF8&qid=1593244938&sr=8-5

Kindle version:
https://www.amazon.com/Wings-Ideas-Gabriella-Balcom-
ebook/dp/B08B8YGTBJ/ref=mp_s_a_1_5?
dchild=1&keywords=Gabriella+Balcom&qid=1593244938&s
r=8-5

Here are some reader comments about the book:

"I loved each of these stories."

"...great job putting unique twists...highly recommend..."

"A Time of Reckoning was a sweet delight."

"Her Only Desire...really touched my heart."

"Each adventure is an easy read and thought provoking.
Quite the journey."

"...great creation...five senses are tickled and tantalized...I
was intrigued from the beginning to the end."

"...a Mini Masterwork in the Horror Genre."

"Nun or Not? … a true work of art… Can be read again and
again with pleasure...I cannot recommend this tale more
highly; setting, character and structure work like a piece of
music to produce a mini-symphony that reverberates with
beauty with each reading."

Gabriella Balcom

Worth Waiting For

Gabriella Balcom's novella was published by
JayZoMon/Dark Myth Company after she won second
place in their 2020 Open Contract Challenge (a competition
in which over hundred authors competed for publishing
contracts and cash prizes) . Here's a little bit about her story:

It's never too late for love, and getting older isn't the end of
life. Sometimes it's just the beginning.

When Wilfred's wife died, he was devastated. Their young
children were, too. He left his military career and raised
them alone, never regretting his choices. Days stretched
into weeks, months, and years. By the time his children
finished college and moved out, his routines were set in
stone—work, hobbies, work... Coworkers had questioned
the lack of a woman in Wilfred's life, trying again and again
to set him up on dates, but he'd resisted every time. Starting
a new relationship would've been a betrayal of his deceased
spouse, and being single was the norm for him. Being single
was comfortable.

Eventually, he moves to a new place, and a sweet lady stops
by to welcome him to the neighborhood.

Wilfred never dreamed he was lonely—not until Sadie
came to his door.

Down with the Sickness and Other Chilling Tales

Worth Waiting For is available at:

https://www.amazon.com/Worth-Waiting-Gabriella-Balcom-ebook/dp/B08NXYGPDD/

Readers made the following comments:

"...I love this so much..."

"A sweet story of love and companionship...nicely written."

"The characters are real, it's emotional, and well written...I would recommend it to any romance reader"

"Great story"

Gabriella Balcom

The Return

The world doesn't know about the compound hidden underground, and the wealthy investors funding it want things to stay as they are. It's 2030, and scientists have made numerous scientific advances. They use cutting-edge technology with their feline service units and Human Replicas—HRs, as they're commonly known. However, most of the research being conducted in the facility is illegal. If animal rights' activists had an inkling of what went on, they'd clamor for justice. Human rights' activists would scream from the rooftops.

The HRs are virtual prisoners with no rights and more and more of them are dying. Needless to say, they dream of freedom. Surprisingly, one of the top facility scientists isn't happy, either. Tensions are mounting, and things are not as they appear.

The Return is available at:

https://bit.ly/39y9iOL

Reader comments about Gabriella's book:

"...This is a thrilling ride...I'm hoping there's a sequel."

"...man, it got me good. Best plot twist I've read in a book...you'll love this book!"

"Fascinating and amazing."

"...had me on the edge of my seat."

Down with the Sickness and Other Chilling Tales

Free's Tale: No Home at Christmas-time

Humans aren't the only ones who dream. Dogs do, too.

Christmas is coming, but Free isn't anywhere close to being happy. He's dreamed of a loving home forever, but knows his chances of ever having one are slim to nonexistent. A mean man kicks him and chases him with a broom. Terrified, he flees, stumbles into a large hole filled with water, and looks like the Mud Monster from Hell when he emerges, the goop encrusting his body starting to freeze. He aches all over, his entire body feels frozen, and he's barely able to remain on his feet.

But then Free runs into a group of larger dogs, and wonders if he's about to die.

Free's Tale: No Home at Christmas-time is available at:

https://www.amazon.com/dp/B08R2DW2N2

Reader comments about Gabriella Balcom's story:

"A sweet and charming tale you'll just eat up..."

"Perfect for any dog lover!"

"I cried, but they were good tears..."

"Beautiful...I couldn't stop reading."

Gabriella Balcom

Publications Featuring Gabriella Balcom's Works

Gabriella has works published or pending publication as follows:

Barrio Blues: Nightmare With a Twist

Black Hare Press: 666, Ancients, Angels, Apocalypse, Area 51,, Beyond, Dark Moments, Deep Underground Series, Eerie Christmas, Envy, Greed, Hate, Jibbernocky, Lockdown anthologies, Love, Lust, Monsters, Nom Nom, Oceans, Pride, Reign, Sloth, Unravel, What If, Worlds, Year One, Year Two

Black Ink Fiction: Blood Lust, Festival of Fear, Halloween Frights, Heartless, Infection, Legends of Night, Movie Madness, New Tales of Old Volume 2, Once Upon a Drabble, Pestilence, Reaper Man, Revelations, Summer Terrors, The Mummy

Blood Song Books: Curses and Cauldrons, Farmhouse Horror, Forest of Fear 1, Forest of Fear 2

Breaking Rules Europe: Lost Lore and Legends

Celestial Echo Press: Twofer Compendium

Clarendon House Publications: Cadence, Fireburst, Galaxy

Down with the Sickness and Other Chilling Tales

2, Glamour, Gleam, Gold, Miracle, On the Wings of Ideas, Poetica, Poetica 2, Poetica 3, Poetica 4, Poetica 6, Rapture, Tempest, Vortex, Window, and more.

Crow's Feet Journal: Up On The House Top

Dastaan World: Athena, Her Only Desire, Disturbia, Justified, and more

Dragon Soul Press: Organic Ink #1, Organic Ink #2

Eerie River Publishing: Forgotten Ones

Eleanor Merry: Dark Halloween, Dark Xmas, Extreme Drabbles, Supernatural Drabbles of Dread

Fantasia Divinity Magazine and Publishing: Burning Dreams, Halloween's Fright and Autumn's Delight, Summer's Splash, The Best of 2020, Waters of Destruction, Winds of Despair, Wishes of Illusion, and more

Horror Tree: Unholy Trinity

Inner Circle Writer's Group Magazine: works in a few issues

Insignia Press: Mythical Beings, Mythical Creatures

Gabriella Balcom

Iron Faerie Publishing: The Best of 2020, Daily Flights of Fantasy, Gods and Goddesses, Ivy & Sage, Rowan and Oak

JayZoMon/Dark Myth Publications: Worth Waiting For

John F. Green, editor: Tales of the Southwest

Lulu.com: Share Your Scare

Paper Dijnn Press: Dawn, Lyric, Terror, Trepidation and Touches of Hope, and several publications on Djinn World

Penned in the City: Unity

Pixie Forest Publishing: Dark Descending, Magical Reality, Phobia

Raven and Drake: Aliens, Candy Capers

Reanimated Writers Press: 100 Word Zombie Bites

Scout Media and Music: A Contract of Words

Siren's Call Publications: various stories

Soteira Press: Horror USA: California, Horror USA: Texas

123

Down with the Sickness and Other Chilling Tales

Stormy Island Publishing: Sea Glass Hearts

Suicide House Publishing: Scary Snippets Christmas, Scary Snippets Halloween, Scary Snippets Valentine's Day

Sweetycat Press: A Love Letter (or Poem) to…, I, The Writer, In A Flash, Movement, Stories And Poems In The Song Of Life, The Book of Books, The Poetics, To Be Or Not To Be A Writer, Who's Who Among Emerging Writers 2020, Who's Who Among Emerging Writers 2021

The Great Void: Black Veins, Blood Crown

The World of Myth Magazine: works in numerous issues

Writers Journey Blog: Journeys

Zombie Pirate Publishing: Flash Fiction Addiction, Phuket Tattoo

———————